FATAL ENCOUNTER

WAR GIRL SERIES BOOK 6

MARION KUMMEROW

Fatal Encounter

Marion Kummerow

CONTENTS

WARSAW MAP

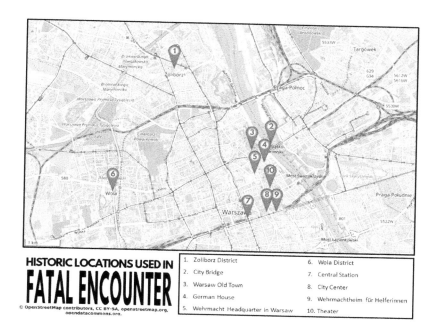

© OpenStreetMap contributors

CHAPTER 1

Warsaw, May 1944

Lotte stepped off the train, excitement about her new life burning in her chest. Holding the paper with instructions in her hand, she made her way to the *Wehrmachtheim für Helferinnen*, the dormitory for the female Wehrmacht auxiliaries in Warsaw, Poland.

She walked the three blocks from the central train station with her small suitcase in hand. The spring sun shone down on her, casting the city in a magnificent glimmer while warming the air. Lotte took the bright sunshine as a good omen for the future.

Warsaw was more beautiful than she'd imagined. Certainly in a better state than her beloved hometown, Berlin, reduced to rubble by the constant Allied bombing. Fifteen minutes later she arrived at the building and opened the wooden door.

"Can I help you?" a young woman greeted her in

German. The woman was clad in the *Helferinnen* uniform, consisting of a gray jacket and garrison cap with the Imperial Eagle carrying the swastika. A matching gray skirt, a white blouse with a black tie and black shoes completed the look. Her right sleeve bore the lightning-flash badge identifying her as a signals assistant.

"I was told to come here after I got off the train," Lotte said and added, "My name is Alexandra Wagner and I'm a *Wehrmachthelferin*." She offered the woman the paper containing her orders and tried not to let her nerves get the best of her. So much had happened in the past few months, including having to fake her own death and assume a new identity, but this was a chance to put all of that behind her and make a difference.

"Very good, Alexandra. I'm Karin. We've been waiting for your arrival already. Please follow me."

Lotte followed Karin through the front office, along a long hallway with doors to both sides. They stopped in front of a door with the sign "Office".

"Oberführerin Kaiser will get you all set up. She's the boarding master and our superior for all things apart from our actual working position." Karin lowered her voice to a conspiratorial whisper. "It's best not to get her upset." Then she knocked on the door and moments later a voice from the inside said, "*Herein.*"

"Oberführerin, here's the new arrival," Karin said and dashed off to return to her previous post.

Behind a huge desk sat another uniformed woman, about forty years of age. She stood and stretched out her hand. "Welcome, Helferin Wagner. May I see your orders please?"

Lotte handed them over, slightly confused at being addressed with her new title, instead of the more informal Fräulein. In that moment, her mission suddenly became real to her. It wasn't a game anymore.

The older woman nodded and then stood. "I'll take you to the supply room for outfitting and then have someone show you to the dormitory. While you're not a soldier, you are an official employee of the Wehrmacht and will be expected to act and dress as such at all times."

Lotte followed Frau Kaiser through the maze of hallways, trying not to show her nerves. For now, she'd focus on getting her uniform and figuring out where she was to sleep.

Inside the supply room Oberführerin Kaiser began pulling articles of clothing from shelves and laid several garments on a counter, marking them on her list. Soon one gray dress suit, two white blouses, a black tie, three pairs of ugly woolen socks, a light coat, and a garrison cap lay in front of Lotte.

"You will also be issued a pair of shoes. What size?"

"Thirty-nine," Lotte said.

The Oberführerin retrieved a pair of sturdy black shoes and added them to the pile. "There you go. Please put the uniform on in the changing room over there. I'll wait for you in my office. Will you find the way back?"

"Yes, Oberführerin. Thank you," Lotte said and took her new garments to the small changing room that was more like an oversized closet and slipped them on. She looked at herself in the mirror hanging on the back of the door and stuck out her tongue at the Imperial Eagle adorning her breast pocket.

While she hated the insignia of the Reich, she couldn't help but give a twirl and admire herself in the nifty uniform. Hers didn't have the single-flash badge on the sleeve like Karin's, but a badge with six flashes organized in a circle, identifying her as radio operating personnel.

The skirt hung a bit loose on her bony hips, but with needle and thread, she'd make it fit properly. Returning to glance at herself in the mirror, she donned the garrison cap, adjusting it to the side of her head the way the women on the propaganda posters wore their caps.

Perfect, she thought and for a tiny moment she forgot that she wasn't here to serve the German war effort. Several minutes later she exited the small room and returned to Oberführerin Kaiser's office.

"Everything fits fine," Lotte said after being asked inside.

The other woman looked her up and down and then nodded once. "Very well, Helferin. Go straight through to the door at the end of the hallway. I have assigned you a bunk in dormitory three. I trust you will have no problem finding your way there?"

"I will be able to find my own way. Thank you for your help, Oberführerin."

The woman turned away and Lotte realized she'd been dismissed. She exited the office as quietly as possible and walked down the hallway until she came to the door with the number three on it.

She stepped into a room with four beds, two against each of the side walls, four lockers, one table with two chairs beneath the window, and a washbasin in the corner. Her new quarters were Spartan to say the least, but a huge improvement on the barracks at the concentration camp in Ravensbrück.

Lotte was still contemplating which one of the meticulously made beds belonged to her when the door burst open and two chatting girls stepped inside. They stopped in their tracks when they saw Lotte standing in the middle of the room. From their sleeve badges she could identify one as a signals assistant and the other one as a radio operator like herself.

"Hello, I'm Alexandra Wagner. Oberführerin Kaiser assigned me this room," Lotte said stretching out her hand.

One of the girls, a beautiful brunette, straightened her skirt and giggled, shaking Lotte's hand. "We call her *the Dragon* when she can't hear. You'll soon find out that she lives up to her nickname. I'm Heidi by the way."

The other girl, not older than twenty, with long dark-blonde hair carefully combed into fashionable waves, stepped forward next. "I'm Gerlinde. Nice to meet you." Following Lotte's bewildered glance across the room, she added, "The bunk over there is yours, next to mine. On the other side are Heidi and Karin. You probably met her since she has door duty today."

Heidi pouted, "Another one of the Dragon's inventions. She keeps a list of the times when everyone leaves and returns. A minute late and you're due for kitchen duty or some other nasty task.

"Thanks for the warning," Lotte said and glanced at the two smartly turned out girls, who looked like their biggest sorrow was whether their hairstyle matched the one on the newest fashion magazine.

Lotte herself had never cared much about looking ladylike, preferring plimsolls to pumps. Her own fiery red hair was as untamable as a hurricane and, since joining up, she'd resigned herself to wearing it in one or two plaits to make it look decent.

Discipline, though, wasn't a problem for Lotte. Not anymore. She'd learned it the hard way. The hardest way, actually. In Ravensbrück a woman could get beaten to death for being late or otherwise disobedient. No, Lotte would be the poster child of a *Wehrmachthelferin*.

She stowed her belongings in the locker, while Heidi and Gerlinde tossed questions at her. Lotte carefully navigated the inquiries, sticking to her cover story. "I'm an only child and my parents died a few years back. When I turned eighteen in February, I decided to do my bit for the war effort and joined up. I trained almost three months near Cologne and now I'm here."

"Cologne? That must be so exciting. Tell us how it was. Did you go to dances? Motion pictures? Did you have many suitors?" Gerlinde asked with big, dreamy eyes.

"We weren't actually in Cologne, but a few dozen miles away. And there were no dances." Lotte could only wonder about Gerlinde's naivety. Didn't she have the slightest idea about the desolate state of the city after being the target of hundreds of air raids?

"Have you been here for long?" Lotte asked her new roommates.

"We arrived last week," Heidi said.

"It's incredibly exciting here," Gerlinde added.

"All the dashing soldiers…"

"And the leisure activities…"

"And the dapper uniform…"

"If it weren't for the Dragon, it would be like paradise."

"Paradise?" Lotte inwardly laughed at her overzealous roommates. "And here I thought there was a war going on."

"Pah...the war...the front line is far away and it's so much better here than back home." Heidi sat down on her bed, took lipstick and a hand mirror from her purse and carefully retraced her lips.

"Where are you from?" Lotte asked.

Since Heidi was occupied painting her lips, Gerlinde answered for both of them. "We're from the same village in East Prussia. Our parents are the biggest land owners around there, but instead of letting us go to school in the city of Königsberg, they insisted we stay in the village with private tutors."

Heidi stashed the utensils in her purse, gave an air-kiss and added, "Boring...You have no idea how boring it was. Especially since all the eligible men left to become soldiers. What's a girl got to do without any men about? We couldn't sit around talking to cows, now could we?"

"I guess not," Lotte said, not really paying attention to Heidi's complaints. Despite the fact that Lotte's family wasn't rich, her two roommates reminded her of herself less than a year ago.

Sheltered. Bored. Unaware of what was really going on in this country. One rash decision had sent Lotte's entire world tumbling and almost killed her. She didn't regret her actions, but she regretted not having taken the time to properly think them through – and the fact that her best friend Irmhild had died because of it. Because of her. The feeling of residual guilt threatened to choke her, and she tried to swallow it down.

No. Lotte would never take freedom or life for granted again. Thanks to her sisters, she'd been given a second chance at life and she intended to use it to help end the madness of this war.

"So we joined the Wehrmacht. Why are you here?"

To spy for the Allies. Lotte bit her lip. In her former life as a sheltered adolescent she might have blurted out what was on her mind, but since she'd assumed a fake identity, she weighed every word before she spoke. "Why am I here? To help the war effort of course." The answer didn't seem to satisfy her two new friends and she added, "And for the dapper uniform, too. Don't you think it makes me look like Marika Rökk?"

"Marika Rökk," Heidi squealed. "She must be the best-looking actress in all of the Reich. Even the Führer admires her greatly."

"The uniform does make you look preppy, and all the men will turn their heads after you, you'll see," Gerlinde said, glancing at her elegant wristwatch.

"Let's go and show you around Warsaw, then we can have dinner in the mess with the boys." Heidi straightened her skirt and stepped in front of the small mirror over the washbasin to adjust her cap.

"Don't you have to work?" Lotte asked.

"No, we finished for today," Gerlinde answered and took her hand. "Come on. We're here to have fun, right?"

"Right." Lotte plastered an enthusiastic smile on her face, even though having fun was the last of her reasons to be here.

The three of them walked along Nowy Świat, New World Street, until Gerlinde stopped in front of a huge and beautiful building and said, "That's the theater. They give performances on the weekend."

Lotte nodded. Apparently this *Wehrmachthelferinnen* job provided one big adventure for the girls, desperate to flee their boring homes or their bombed-out hometowns.

After fifteen minutes of walking they reached the building that served as mess for all German military personnel, including the female staff.

Gerlinde and Heidi greeted a few of the other girls streaming inside and introduced them to Lotte. "Hey, this is Alexandra, our new roommate. She's a radio operator and will start work tomorrow."

The other girls were mostly signals assistants, nurses, and a few radio operators like herself. Everyone talked and laughed, eating amounts of food Lotte hadn't seen for a long time in a country of rations. They searched for an empty table and sat down.

Gerlinde pointed out the abundance of handsome men, all flirtatious and intent on charming the women present. She couldn't stop gushing about how dashing they looked in their uniforms, and drew her fair share of attention and inviting glances from across the room.

Lotte watched with a jaded eye, caring not for how cocky these men behaved, nor the reactions of the women. At home she had heard wild stories about the loose morals of the Helferinnen, who were often nicknamed *Blitzmädel*, flash girls, not only for the flash badges on their sleeves, but also for the speed some of them ended up in bed with one of the officers.

Lotte, for one, didn't have any intention of living up to that image; she had more important things on her mind.

Oberführerin Kaiser had instructed them that walking out with one of the soldiers wasn't well received. She wouldn't give her superiors the slightest reason to be dissatisfied with her work or her person.

"The men here are so good-looking," Gerlinde gushed on the way home.

"I didn't really notice," Lotte said.

Gerlinde shook her head at her and asked, "You didn't notice? Were your eyes closed?"

"No, I guess I'm just excited to get to work," Lotte answered, fighting a wave of nostalgia. After last year's events, she would never be so jaunty again.

"Well, that's what tomorrow is for," Heidi said and opened the wooden door of the dormitory building for them. Oberführerin Kaiser was already waiting near the entrance, taking note of who returned home at what time.

About an hour later, the four girls crawled between the sheets. Lotte doused the light, but even though her roommates fell into a deep sleep minutes later, she lay awake for several hours, thinking about the future. She was excited to get started on her new life, but also scared.

Very scared.

CHAPTER 2

Peter Wolf pushed his way through the crowd, trying to find empty seats on the train.

"Up here," he called out to his wife, her sister and her mother, indicating a compartment with four vacant seats. He blocked the door with his broad shoulders to prevent others from pushing inside. Minutes later everyone in their party was finally seated.

"I had no idea the trains would be this crowded," Frau Klausen, his mother-in-law, said.

"It's been like this for quite a while. Since they started using all passenger trains for troop transports," Ursula, Peter's sister-in-law, answered.

"...and requisitioning all private vehicles for the war effort," his wife, Anna, added.

"It's a miracle we even got the travel permits for all of us," Peter said, helping the heavily pregnant Ursula out of her light summer coat and heaving up the heavy suitcases into the overhead bin.

"Well, we are going to attend a special Nazi ceremony, so it's not like we're traveling for pure pleasure." Anna pursed her lips as she said the words. Peter knew how much his wife hated the Nazis for everything they'd done to her family.

"I'm so happy you girls could come with me to visit Lydia; it'll be a much-needed reprieve from the air raids in Berlin for all of us," Frau Klausen said as the train started moving. "May I sit over there? I get sick when sitting with my back to the direction of train."

Peter got up and changed places with her. Now he sat opposite Anna and couldn't hold her hand during the trip, but he had the pleasure of looking into her beautiful face with the dark blue eyes, framed by shining blonde hair. Warmth spread throughout his body. As far as he was concerned, admiring her was as enjoyable as holding her hand. He was a truly lucky fellow to have found love again, after his first wife was killed – back when he still went by the name of Piotr Zdanek.

Ursula, one year older than Anna, had the same blue eyes and blonde hair, but instead of Anna's straight strands, natural waves fell about her face and shoulders. At least he assumed so, because what knowledge did he have about the little tricks women used to make their faces and hair look elegant, yet natural? Anna and Ursula were the spitting image of their mother, who must have looked like them twenty-five years ago.

Caught in his thoughts, he followed the conversation of the women only with half an ear. He was worried about the happenings in the European war theater. Through his clandestine contacts with the British, he knew there was something big about to happen in his home country, Poland. But nobody knew the precise details.

"...I haven't been to Kleindorf in years." Anna's sweet voice caught his attention and a smile spread across his face.

"Tell me what it's like at your Aunt Lydia's," he said.

"To cite our baby sister Lotte, it's boooooring." Anna laughed. "The village where Aunt Lydia's farm lies doesn't even have a train station. We'll have to take the bus from Mindelheim to get to Kleindorf. From there it's another twenty minutes' walk to her farm."

"I arranged for her to pick up our luggage with an ox cart," Frau Klausen said, winking at Peter. He didn't shy away from hard work, but the prospect of not having to lug all their suitcases to the farm still sent a jolt of relief through him.

At every stop more and more people pushed inside, filling the two remaining seats in their compartment, and also piling in the corridor, making a trip to the bathroom next to impossible. About halfway to Munich, where they had to change trains, the rail car became so crowded no new passengers could climb aboard the train and people started pushing through the windows. At least fifteen passengers filled their compartment to the brim, everyone desperate to get wherever they needed to go.

"It's very hot in here," Ursula murmured quietly, not one to complain when nothing could be done.

"Here, have some water," Anna said, offering her a flask.

Ursula took it, drank a small amount and then handed it back. "Thank you."

Peter glanced at Ursula, who looked very pale, except for red, heated cheeks. She held her hands across her belly, as if protecting the child inside from accidental bumps of the standing passengers. He got up from his seat by the open window to change places with her and said, "Sit here."

"Thanks," Ursula said and fanned herself with cooler air from outside.

After endless hours, they finally arrived in Munich and changed into a slightly less crowded regional train bound for Mindelheim. When at last they reached Mindelheim, Aunt Lydia was waiting for them at the platform, much to their surprise.

"Aunt Lydia," Anna called out, waving to gain her attention. She pushed her way through the crowded platform, leaving Peter to trail after the women, his hands full of luggage.

"Lydia, you came all the way here. We could have taken the bus," Frau Klausen said, greeting her sister.

"Frida. It's so good to see you. I'm so glad you could all come." Lydia gave her sister a short embrace before she looked at her nieces. "Anna, Ursula. It's been how long? Four years? Or longer?"

"I believe almost five years, ever since this war started," Ursula answered.

"Aunt Lydia, this is my husband, Peter," Anna said.

"Peter, welcome to Bavaria. Such a shame that I couldn't attend your wedding," the older woman said with a smile shaking his hand.

"Thank you, Frau Meier," Peter said. Lydia was about his age, but since she was his mother-in-law's sister, he opted for the more formal greeting.

"Please, call me Lydia. Come. We have to catch the bus." Lydia hurried them on and led the way outside the tiny train station to the place where the bus already waited to pick up the disembarking passengers. At the bus stop in Kleindorf, Lydia's oldest son, Jörg, who'd just turned eleven years old, waited for them with a rickety-looking ox-driven cart. Somehow, they managed to fit everyone plus their suitcases onto the cart and shortly thereafter they stopped in front of a very tidy-looking farmhouse.

Lydia showed them their rooms and asked them to come down into the kitchen for dinner. As Peter carried the suitcases upstairs with Jörg's help, the boy stopped for a moment before entering the small room assigned to Peter and Anna. "This one used to be Lotte's, God bless her."

"I'm sure she's better off where she is now," Peter said in a serious tone. Nobody except for immediate family knew that Lotte wasn't really dead but had assumed the fake identity of Alexandra Wagner. Despite the obvious grief in the boy's eyes, it was best not to let him in on the secret. When Jörg left, Peter closed the door and wrapped Anna in his arms.

"It's true, you know," she murmured against his shoulder.

"What?"

"Wherever Lotte is, she's better off than in Ravensbrück."

"It's over. She's safe now." He hugged Anna tighter, a stab cutting into his heart at the lie. He'd only seen her little sister Lotte once, at their wedding ceremony. And he'd never approved of Lotte's plan to become a spy for the Allies. Especially not when she'd told them she was being deployed to Warsaw. As much as he loved his hometown, the Polish capital wasn't a safe place to be right now, not when world-changing events loomed in the air.

"You're right. Let's go downstairs and introduce you to everyone." Anna gave him a kiss, before she straightened her skirt and led him to the kitchen, where Lydia and her six children waited for them. Lydia's husband had been on furlough several weeks ago, on his way from somewhere in Serbia to France. Rumors had it that the Allies would try to invade France, so Hitler had transferred huge numbers of troops to the West.

"Dinner is ready. Wash your hands and sit," Lydia told the children and showed the visitors where to sit. Peter admired the woman in her thirties who managed not only her six children, all under the age of twelve, but also an entire farm, without the help of her conscripted husband. But then he shouldn't be surprised; his Anna and the other Klausen women were forces to be reckoned with.

"Lydia, this dinner is exceptional," Frau Klausen praised her sister.

"It definitely is. I believe I haven't eaten such a delicious meal in ages," Peter added. With the rationing, they rarely got fresh vegetables or milk, but here on the farm, food didn't seem as much of an issue as it was in the city.

"Thank you for having me," Peter said later, while Anna and the girls cleared the dishes from the table. Ursula excused herself, as she was tired from the trip, but he and Frau Klausen sat with Lydia in the sitting room.

"You are very welcome. Thank you for bringing my sister and my nieces here to celebrate with me. I know how difficult it is to travel these days."

"It was good to get out of the city."

"We hear so many bad things about the air raids. I'm glad we live far enough from the big cities that we rarely see an enemy aircraft." Lydia poured him and her sister a glass of self-brewed schnapps.

"That's good," Peter said as the clear liquid ran down his throat. "When is the ceremony?"

"The day after tomorrow. On Mother's Day." Lydia gave a curt laugh. "The Nazis are pulling out all the stops on this. There's a festival with music and parades, and the mayor of Mindelheim, Herr Keller, will give a speech. Then someone from the propaganda ministry will award the cross of honor to all Aryan mothers who have at least four children."

"Since Lydia has just borne her sixth child, she'll receive the Silver Cross," Frau Klausen said.

"I could do without it," Lydia said, lulling her baby to sleep, "but the Silver Cross is very prestigious and grants me special status as *honorable mother*. I'd rather not go to the ceremony, but since the unfortunate events with Lotte, I'm grateful for any help remaining in good standing with the administration and Herr Keller. The award provides insurance for me, and I'll put a good face on the matter."

Peter nodded, empathy for Lydia filling his soul. He'd been curious as to why the family had made such a fuss about attending the ceremony. But now he understood. The mayor had cast an eye on Lydia's farm, and only waited for an opportunity to take it from her. But he wouldn't be able to touch the bearer of a Silver Mother's Cross. He would first have to deprive her of the award.

"Do you mind if I retire?" Lydia asked them. "I have to put the children to bed and the cows need milking early in the morning." Suddenly, she looked tired.

Frau Klausen waved her off. "We've got this. Anna and I will finish doing the dishes. We don't want to be a burden on you."

"Thank you, dear. I'm glad you're all here. I'll see you both in the morning." Lydia cradled the baby in her arms and walked into the kitchen to order her children to bed. Later, Anna came into the sitting room and asked Peter if he wanted to go for a walk. At this time of the year, the daylight lasted until well into the night, and he agreed. A romantic evening walk with his wife was something they got to do much too infrequently.

Anna linked arms with him and led him around the vast farm, pointing out the barn, the cowshed, and several of the fields. His heart grew weary and he became ever more silent.

As they returned to the farmhouse, she stopped to ask, "What does that look on your face mean?"

"It's just...it reminds me of home." A wave of nostalgia swept over him as he remembered the happy times during his childhood on his grandparents' farm near Lodz. But that had happened in another lifetime. Before he met his first wife Ludmila and moved to Warsaw. Before he joined the Polish Army. Before Hitler invaded and Peter fled with his unit via Romania and Iran to Britain to join the British Army.

And before the Nazis killed Ludmila and his son Janusz. Because they were Jews.

≈

On Sunday morning everyone was giddy to attend the event, but for different reasons. Lydia's children welcomed the distraction from day-to-day life, since festivities and happy celebrations came few and far between. The adults, though, loathed the *Hitlerjugend* parades and propaganda speeches that had to be endured first.

Peter escorted Anna to the marketplace in Mindelheim, where hundreds of people had already gathered. Lydia seemed to know every last person and they stopped to greet far too many people for Peter to even try to remember.

The marketplace had been decorated with festive red and white ribbons, and the swastika flag hung from virtually every window. On one side of the marketplace a wooden dais had been erected where currently a group of girls from the *Jungmädelbund*, the Hitler Youth for girls under fifteen, performed gymnastic exercises.

They ended their performance with thundering applause from the spectators. Most of the girls rushed to their parents, their faces heated with sweat and pride. Then, an official in a decorated uniform, whom Lydia identified as the mayor, party leader and chief of police, Herr Keller, stepped on the dais.

Peter noticed a shudder rip through Anna, despite the wonderful sunny day, and he wrapped an arm around her shoulders.

"He's the one…" she whispered.

"Shush," Peter put a finger on her lips to keep her from saying anything compromising.

The mayor gave a lengthy speech about the virtues of the German Mother, reminding everyone that today was a day of happiness and celebration, despite the sacrifices that some had to make. Peter looked around, seeing more than one woman secretly dabbing at her eyes. In the past years, with all the fallen soldiers, Mother's Day had become a sad occasion for so many of them.

"...the war of birthing has to continue. It's every pure German mother's duty to birth children for the Reich and the Führer. You cannot let insecurity and the vile attacks of our enemies let you waver in your efforts to produce soldiers for our great army..."

Peter tuned out the disgusting words of the mayor. What woman would feel compelled to have a child just to send it to die in the next war the Nazis were obviously already planning? And without their husbands? As far as he was concerned, a man was needed to conceive the child, but the number of men attending the celebration was minimal. The Nazis probably already worked on some wicked solution for this conundrum.

Anna elbowed him. "Where are your thoughts?"

He gave a rueful grimace and watched as an official from the Propaganda Ministry climbed the dais and started to read the names of the women to be awarded the Mother's Cross in Bronze, for giving the Führer four racially pure, genetically fit, healthy children.

Next were the Silver Awards, for having borne six children, and Frau Klausen had to nudge her sister forward when her name was called. Clapping and cheering accompanied the women as they approached the dais. The official proceeded to give the award to the women lining up, shook their hands and ended his congratulations with the words, "The Child ennobles the Mother."

Lydia stepped down and returned to her family with the

cross hanging from her neck, while the tribute to the mothers with the Gold Cross for eight children continued. Lydia's girls wanted to touch the award, and she handed it around for everyone to appreciate.

For the girls it seemed to be nothing more than a fancy, glittery necklace, the Nazi symbolism meaningless, which they would love to use in their games.

It was the first time Peter had got a glimpse of such an award from up close. It resembled a Marian Cross, with the swastika on the front, surrounded by enamel blue and white. The inscription around the swastika said *Der Deutschen Mutter*, for the German Mother. It was fastened on a long blue and white ribbon to be worn around the neck.

"Can we play now?" three-year-old Maria asked.

Since the official part of the celebration had ended, Lydia allowed her children to take off to play. A marching band of Hitler Youth boys occupied the dais and played popular songs. Despite the festivities' being sponsored by the Nazis, Peter enjoyed the cheerful atmosphere and soon followed the example of a few couples and danced with Anna.

The war had made things so difficult, the jubilant mood of the day was a welcome respite.

CHAPTER 3

L otte sat in the transmission room in the building next to the *Oberfeldkommandantur,* the German Wehrmacht headquarters in Warsaw. She'd practiced hard to master the Morse code during her training, but real -life transmission was a different monster. During the first week of work, she left the transmission room every day with a pounding head and bleeding fingers.

"School was so much easier," she complained to Gerlinde, who occupied the workstation beside hers, during a break.

"I know…it was like twenty minutes of Morse work and then something else. Not eight hours straight like here. My first week was brutal, but you'll get used to it. I promise."

Just as Gerlinde had predicted, in the second week work had already become a challenging but manageable task. Over the weekend, calluses had grown on Lotte's fingertips and her brain had adapted to the required focus. Every day they received phone calls from several locations across

Poland and Russia, and the group of radio operators translated this information into Morse code and relayed it to the armed forces high command in Berlin.

During the first week she'd worked side by side with a supervisor, making sure her transmissions were accurate, but now she sat alone at her desk, trying to memorize all the information about directions, troop movements, and everything else that might prove vital for the Allies. But first she needed to visit her contact person.

This evening, Lotte sought out Oberführerin Kaiser in her office. Since the Wehrmacht encouraged her female auxiliaries to engage in cultural activities in their leisure time, she hoped Frau Kaiser would agree with her request. Despite being called the Dragon, the woman was actually very benevolent towards her subordinates – as long as they stuck to her rules.

"Oberführerin, may I ask for something?"

The older woman looked up from her desk, "Yes, Helferin Wagner, what is it?"

"Since I enjoyed the weekly folkloric evening with the traditional German songs so much, I would like to take up piano classes," Lotte said.

"You liked our folkloric evening?" Oberführerin Kaiser beamed with pride.

"Yes."

"It is a shame not more young women think like you. Our cultural heritage is an important factor in racial purity and the superiority of the Master Race. Once we have won this war, you girls will go back to your families and raise your many children with the Führer's ideals in mind."

Lotte dutifully nodded, although she didn't have the

slightest intention of raising her future children according to Hitler's ideals. "I believe the piano lessons will help me to understand more of our great cultural heritage. Just imagine being able to play the magnificent music by the three master composers Ludwig van Beethoven, Richard Wagner and Anton Bruckner."

The Oberführerin beamed, a pleased smile on her usually strict face. "Music is so important, Helferin Wagner. I'm glad you show such enthusiasm, and obviously I approve of the piano lessons. Do you want me to find a suitable teacher for you?"

Lotte's heart thumped painfully in her throat and she took a moment to breathe before she answered, "Actually, I was recommended a teacher already. Her name is Ewa Gusten. She's a *Volksdeutsche* and sometimes performs at the theater."

"Well then. Once a week and be home before curfew. But be warned...if your work suffers, I will revoke the permit."

"It won't. Thank you so much, Oberführerin," Lotte said and left the office. She rushed to her room and fell on her bed, soaked with cold sweat, but exhilarated at taking another step toward her clandestine job as spy.

Ewa was much more than a pianist and music teacher. She belonged to the Polish Home Army, a major resistance organization, and was in direct contact with an agent for the British SOE. During Lotte's time hiding out at the convent, she'd met a man who worked for the SOE and who'd recruited her to become a spy for the British. It had been his suggestion to join up and become a radio operator.

The next evening, she went to the address where Ewa lived and knocked on the door.

"Yes?" came a female voice from behind the closed door.

"Good afternoon, I was told I could take piano lessons here. I'm an adult but a fast learner," Lotte responded with the required coded sentence.

The door opened and a woman in her forties with dark brown hair and brilliant brown eyes peeked out to make sure Lotte was alone, before inviting her inside. "Come in." The woman closed and locked the door and led the way deeper into the apartment. "You must be Alexandra. You've started work?"

"Yes." Lotte offered her a small smile and stated needlessly, "Our coded phrase worked."

"Of course, it did." Ewa smiled.

"My superior actually liked the idea. She thinks every woman should know about the finer arts to entertain guests," Lotte said, grimacing.

"Then this will be the perfect cover for your visits. Sit down." Ewa pointed at the stool in front of a shining black piano.

"What?" Lotte's eyes went wide.

"For the cover to work, we must produce results. Did you take lessons as a child?"

Lotte pulled a face but nodded. "I did, but I hated it. I never had the patience to practice long enough to improve."

"Well, let's get started. If anyone ever follows you or asks you to demonstrate how your lessons are progressing, you'll have something to show them." Ewa pulled out a sheet of music and set it on the piano stand.

Lotte groaned, but Ewa's explanation made perfect sense. "Fine. I guess I will be reliving my childhood."

"It will be painless, I promise. Is there a piano to practice on at your dormitory?"

"Not at the dormitory, but at the German House in the Saxon Gardens. I guess I could practice there." Lotte sighed and dutifully put her fingers on the keys to demonstrate what she remembered from her former classes, but her mind went blank. "They change the radio frequency and encryption code every week."

"Then you should come here every week with the new codes. Now, play this." At first sight it looked like a very simple piece of music, but it was hard enough that Lotte shook her head after a long moment studying the paper.

"I'm afraid I can't. I might remember how to play a scale..." Lotte placed her hands on the keys and haltingly managed to play the C major scale. Under Ewa's encouragement Lotte focused on her fingers on the keys and forgot about everything else around her.

"So, do you have anything for me?" Ewa asked after a while.

"What?"

"Information." Ewa smiled. "I always get lost in the music, too. It's my escape from the world."

"Oh yes..." Lotte said and then recounted all the details she remembered from last week's transmissions. At the end of their class, she handed Ewa a piece of paper with her personal sign, code and frequency.

"That's perfect. Now we'll be able to listen in to your radio transmissions, and don't have to wait until you come here." Ewa accompanied her to the door and handed her a sheet of music. "Try to practice as much as you can. You'll see with time you'll come to love the piano."

As Lotte fell asleep later that night, she did so with a big smile upon her face. Learning to play the piano wasn't the worst sacrifice. She'd always loved listening to the instrument and had regretted that she'd not had enough discipline when she was younger to stick with her practice.

Now, it seemed, her life was coming around full circle and she was being given a second chance. Courtesy of the Nazis. She wouldn't thank them for it, but she would apply herself and learn as much as possible during the time she had.

CHAPTER 4

Peter glanced at Ursula, slightly shaking his head at the stubborn woman.

"No. And this is my last word," Ursula said.

"Ursula, but why on earth won't you stay here?" Lydia asked, a pleading tone in her voice. Peter knew why but couldn't very well confront her with her work for the underground network; at least, not where Lydia or the children could hear.

"Because I'm needed in Berlin." Ursula pushed out her lip and put a hand on her hip, before she flinched with pain and smoothed her hand across her huge belly. By the looks of it, the baby could come anytime now, although it wasn't due for another two weeks.

"Ursula, that is not what is best for you or the baby," her mother commented. "Why must you be so stubborn?"

"It's not stubbornness," Ursula defended herself.

"Of course it is," her mother said. "Here, there are no bombs going off at all hours of the night. There is plenty of food, and you couldn't have a better person to help you through the delivery and the first few weeks in handling a newborn than Lydia."

"I know what you say is true, but I still…"

"What? You will be all alone once you return to Berlin," Frau Klausen said.

"I will still have you and Anna…"

"But we won't be there all the time. I'm not even living in the apartment anymore, and Mutter has to go to work. What if you need help in the middle of the night?" Anna looked to Peter for help.

So far, he'd stayed out of the conversations, leaving the arguing to the women, but since they would leave the next day, it was about time to take a stand. He asked, "Ursula, you want to have a healthy baby, yes?"

"Of course I do." Ursula cast him an angry stare, which didn't faze him in the least. He'd stood up to worse opponents than a stubborn woman.

"Then, do what's best not only for the baby, but also the mother. Your baby could come at any time. On the train ride home. In the middle of a bombing attack. Then what? Can you deliver your own baby?"

He watched Ursula's face fall and saw the supportive nod Anna gave him. He was finally getting through to her common sense. "We're not suggesting you stay in Kleindorf indefinitely, just until after the baby is born and strong enough to make the train ride back to Berlin. A couple of months at most."

Ursula looked around the table and stopped at her aunt. "Are you sure I wouldn't be a burden?

Lydia smiled and shook her head. "You will be an added

part of our lives. Stay. Please."

"Fine. For the good of my baby, I will stay here, but for no more than a few months. I wish to be back in Berlin before summer is over."

Lydia patted her niece's arm, "You're making the right decision. And you're not a burden. On the contrary, you can keep an eye on baby Rosa, which gives me more time to work on the fields. Now that summer and harvest is coming, I need all the help I can get."

The next day they said tearful goodbyes before Jörg took them to the train station in Mindelheim with the ox-driven cart.

Ursula whispered just loud enough for Anna and Peter to hear, "If Tom somehow shows up in Berlin looking for me, will you let him know where I am?" Tom was a British RAF pilot whom Ursula had helped escape from Germany – and the father of her baby.

"Off course I will, although I doubt he'll drop from the skies a second time," Anna said. The two sisters exchanged hugs and kisses as if they'd never see each other again. Peter took a step back and raised his hands, fearful Ursula would do the same to him.

"Don't be afraid, Peter," Anna teased him.

"Write every week," Frau Klausen said. "And give us a telephone call when the baby arrives."

"We will," Lydia assured her sister. "Don't worry. Ursula is in good hands with me." For a moment a shadow passed over her face and Peter wondered whether she was thinking about Lotte. The youngest, rebellious Klausen sister had stayed with Lydia for almost two years, before one well-meaning but rash decision had almost cost the young woman her life.

The first part of their journey was uneventful, but when they had to change trains in Munich, the wagons were even more congested than on their outward journey. Peter pushed and shoved inside the train, finding only standing room in one of the compartments. Anna and her mother followed him, sitting down on their suitcases for the next several hours.

He was relieved that he didn't have to worry about keeping another woman safe on this return leg of their trip. Truth be told, he'd been horrified by the possibility that Ursula might deliver during the journey. Birthing was women's domain, one that no man should be forced to witness.

Three times the train had to stop because of an impending air raid, and everyone disembarked, seeking cover in the nearby bushes. When they finally arrived in Berlin Peter was exhausted, hungry and in a bad mood.

The next day he returned to his work as driver for Professor Scherer, a renowned scientist in the fields of medicine and genetics. The British SOE had arranged for him to work for the professor, who entertained contacts with the who's who in Germany. Professor Scherer's house provided a constant meeting place for important politicians, scientists and artists. Being the Professor's right hand had given Peter a firsthand view of things discussed off the record – which he dutifully transmitted to London.

He'd always considered his spying activities important,

but recently he felt a strange restlessness. He should *fight*, instead of sitting around transmitting messages.

For so many years, he'd been hiding out with a false identity, telling himself he was of better use to Poland as a British spy than in a German POW camp. But many of his friends had chosen a different path and stayed in Poland, going underground to join the Home Army and fighting the Nazis every day with partisan activities.

Their efforts had been but a drop in the ocean against the overwhelming German military power suppressing the country. But now, change crackled in the air. In January, Home Army units had joined forces with the Red Army to defeat the Germans, and town after town was being freed from the occupation. Unfortunately, the friendship between the life-long enemies hadn't lasted long and soon after every victory, the Home Army forces were disarmed and sent to Russian labor camps or forced to join the Red Army.

Nevertheless, since Stalin was an ally of the British, a country who'd guaranteed – but not kept their promise – to stand by Poland in case of an invasion by Hitler, Russia was the lesser evil compared to Germany.

Peter maintained contact not only with the British SOE, but also the Polish government in exile in London, and former friends now in the Home Army, so he had a pretty clear picture what was going on in his fatherland. While he pondered his next steps, something happened that changed everything.

On June 6th, the Allies launched a massive attack by landing over twenty thousand troops on the shores of Normandy, France. Goebbels' propaganda ministry down-played the events, talking about "minor fighting" in the radio broadcasts to the populace. But Peter had learned to read between the lines. If Goebbels even admitted to the fighting, it must be huge. As the days and weeks passed it became clear that the Allies were on track to liberate France and the Low Countries.

Peter decided to take matters into his own hands and transmitted a message to London, expressing his desire to go to Poland and fight in liberating his country.

The next day he received the answer:

Do not leave your position.

He uttered a few curses, crumpled the piece of paper and tossed it against the wall. His head sunk onto the desk in despair, and that was how Anna found him much later.

"Darling, what happened?" When he didn't answer, she scanned the room, walked over to the wall, flattened the paper and read it. "What does this mean?" she asked, fear evident in her voice.

"It means that I'm staying in Berlin."

"You never told me you were supposed to leave," Anna said.

"I wasn't."

"And you're not going to give me any further explanation, right?"

He looked at her, suddenly feeling the burden of the entire world on his shoulders. "I...I have this feeling that I need to do something more important than transmitting messages to London. I feel like a coward hiding out here in Berlin while my comrades are sacrificing their lives for our country." Anna's nose turned pale and he hated himself for telling her. She shouldn't have to worry about him. Especially not since London had just told him to stay in his position.

"You're not a coward staying here…" she said.

"No. Let's forget about it." He stood and wrapped his arms around her, placing a kiss on her lips. "How about I take you out to the motion pictures tonight?"

She tried a small smile. "That sounds fine."

CHAPTER 5

June brought wonderful summer days to Warsaw, and every day Lotte felt more at ease with her work as a radio operator. Like clockwork she visited Ewa every week, and to further her cover she'd secured permission to use the piano at the German House to practice. Much to her surprise she started to like playing the instrument. The Nazi-approved classical music had a soothing effect on her, and when she sat at the piano, she didn't think about the war. It was her small escape from reality.

She soon gathered a few admirers among the soldiers who would linger in the hall when she played, but she turned down all their advances. Regardless, her time was filled with social activities. Apart from the weekly folkloric evenings that Oberführerin Kaiser organized, the *Blitzmädel* were encouraged to take part in sports and cultural activities.

Life in Warsaw didn't change much, even after the landing of the Allies in France. It was almost surreal, and sometimes Lotte forgot a war was being waged outside. The bombers didn't shell the city in their nightly raids. Food was never an issue, and the Wehrmacht employees often dined out in restaurants, eating delicacies that hadn't been seen in Germany for years.

One day, Gerlinde rushed into their room, asking, "Will you come with us to the Vistula River?"

"Always," Lotte smiled. Strolling along the river shore was one of her favorite pastimes. The wide river ran the length of the city, surrounded on both sides by sandy banks and greenery that encouraged strolling about.

"Alexandra, some of us are going to the opera tomorrow night. The Dragon already approved and gave us a pass to return home after curfew. Will you come with us?" Gerlinde said as they sat down on the beach, looking across the water.

"That sounds exciting. I would love to," Lotte answered.

"We're going to have dinner out at a restaurant that everyone has been talking about before we go to the opera. It should be a fun evening."

Lotte nodded, but as always when food was involved, she was puzzled at how there could be so much good food available in Warsaw when people in Berlin and other places inside Germany had to make do on meager rations. She could only wonder where all this food came from. The ration cards were generous, and there was always more than enough in the mess to feed everyone.

But for now, she didn't want to think about food shortages or the lack thereof. They were on the cusp of a weekend, and she wanted to relax and enjoy herself. The war would still be there come Monday when she returned to her radio station.

"So, who else is going to the opera?" she asked as they made their way back towards their living quarters.

"Several new units arrived a few days ago." Gerlinde brushed an imaginary grain of dust from her impeccable uniform.

"And I imagine you've already made their acquaintance?"

Gerlinde gave her a cocky grin and nodded. "Some of them. They were transferred in from Lodz."

"Lodz?" Lotte said and both women paused. Even in their sheltered position, they'd heard horror stories about the recent closing of the ghetto and rampaging SS brigades.

"I don't think it's true. They're probably just bragging," Gerlinde said, seemingly having read Lotte's mind.

Lotte couldn't fathom why anyone would brag about these horrible atrocities committed in plain daylight – especially if they weren't true. Who would make up those kinds of things? And why? No, from her own experience she believed every single rumor uttered. "You're probably right," Lotte said.

After a lengthy pause, Gerlinde continued speaking, "I met two men, Helmut and his friend, Johann. They are both going with us tomorrow."

"You don't waste any time, do you?" Lotte teased her roommate.

"There is no time to waste. They are here now but could be moved at any time."

Lotte didn't have a response to that because her friend's words rang true. They could all be dead the next day. She was quiet for a moment and then asked, "So, if there are two men joining us tomorrow, I assume you already have your eye on one?"

"Helmut looks so dashing," Gerlinde said with a dreamy voice.

"So, the man I'm supposed to sweet talk is...?" Lotte wrinkled her nose. The whole opera ploy stank. It was nothing more than a double date.

"Johann."

"I'm doing this only so you can walk out with Helmut. But you owe me one," Lotte said.

"Thank you. Thank you. Thank you." Gerlinde fell around Lotte's neck, just as they arrived in front of the dormitory.

Lotte was waiting with Gerlinde outside the German House at the appointed time when two men clad in Wehrmacht uniform strolled up to them. One of them was blond, and slim; the other one had brown hair and was a few inches taller, with broad shoulders.

"The blond is Helmut, the dark one Johann," Gerlinde whispered to her. After the introductions were made, Gerlinde slipped her arm through Helmut's elbow, leaving Lotte to walk beside Johann to the restaurant. The kind yet serious expression on his face made Lotte's mouth go dry.

She attempted to make small talk. "Gerlinde told me you've been transferred in from Lodz? I've heard the city is nice."

"Well, yes. It used to be the heart of the textile industry

in Poland. Most of the factories have been repurposed to produce war material, though," Johann said.

"So why did your unit come here? Weren't you needed there anymore?" Gerlinde had told her that Johann and Helmut belonged to an anti-partisan unit and it seemed strange, because partisans weren't that much of a problem in Warsaw unlike in more rural parts of the country. At least that's what Lotte figured after putting two and two together from the information she'd picked up.

Johann glanced at her with sad eyes. "That's above my pay grade."

"Does it have something to do with closing down the Ghetto?" Lotte asked, hoping to gather information for Ewa.

"How do you know?"

"Everyone here knows. The relocation of close to one hundred thousand people isn't something that can go unnoticed, especially not if you are the one reporting back to OKW every step of it."

"They're only Jews, an inferior race, but—" Johann's eyes lost their shine and his voice became heavy.

Lotte wanted to punch his face. "How many Jews do you know?"

"Not many." His eyes turned dark and she recognized the shadow of carefully hidden pain.

"And how do you know they're all bad?" The words tumbled out of her mouth before her inner voice could tell her this was the exact same behavior that had gotten her into trouble before. "I mean…maybe not all of them are bad?"

Johann stopped walking and looked at her for a very

long moment, making her squirmy all over. "I don't think they're all bad. And I don't think they deserve to be treated worse than animals. They should have left the country when they could." He took a step back, before he said, "For your own good, you should never repeat these things, nor should you ask so many questions."

"I'm sorry. I don't know why I even said it, since I don't like the Jews either. It was a stressful week, I guess," Lotte lied, pondering whether he'd just given her a veiled threat. But his eyes were full of genuine concern for her. She had the strangest feeling that he knew more about the relocations and hated the plight of the Jews. It was only a hunch and she couldn't very well ask him what exactly happened and whether he supported the Nazis' treatment of other races. And he couldn't very well answer her if he indeed did not.

"We all have these doubts once in a while," Johann said, with the slightest trace of a smile. "I was tricked into this double date, but now I'm glad I'm here."

Lotte flushed with heat up to the roots of her hair. "L… let's hurry and catch up with our friends, then."

At the restaurant they ordered their food and she left it to Gerlinde to entertain and charm their companions. Gerlinde completed the task masterfully with her inconsequential talk about the weather, funny anecdotes from the last sports competitions among the stationed personnel and other mundane topics. Lotte though, kept her gaze on her plate, afraid she'd give her confusing emotions away, should Johann smile at her again.

As they left for the opera house, Johann offered her his arm, and Lotte took it without thinking twice. She shouldn't have. Now slaphappy butterflies danced in her stomach, despite her best intentions to feign disinterest.

Not only did he look strikingly dapper, but he also was one of the most mature men she'd met in a very long time. His calm and deliberate demeanor was a welcome reprieve from the boisterous, flirtatious fellows in the garrison. That he was at least ten years older than she only added to the allure, since she found most boys her age boring, immature and self-assertive, not to mention fervent and uncritical supporters of Hitler. At least Johann had shown some reflection on the topic of the Jews and despite being a sergeant with the rank of Feldwebel, he apparently didn't subscribe to committing atrocities in the name of Hitler.

"Good evening, enjoy the performance," an assistant said as he led them to their places in the theater. Germans-only except for the performers, of course, who were Poles.

"Thank you." Johann nodded at the young man and offered Lotte his arm again to lead her through the tier. Her knees became wobbly at his thoughtfulness.

She'd forgotten to ask Gerlinde what opera would be performed and was pleasantly surprised when she found the leaflet on her seat, indicating it was *The Marriage of Figaro* by Wolfgang Amadeus Mozart, a piece she loved because of its beautiful music and the hilarious plot. Much too soon it ended, and Johann and Helmut insisted on walking them back to their dormitory, although the soldiers' quarters were next to the opera house and they would have to walk all the way back again.

"It's not safe for you two alone after curfew," Johann said with a tone that didn't allow protest. Not that either Gerlinde or Lotte would have protested. Lotte didn't believe it was any more dangerous to walk Warsaw at night than during the day, with German soldiers posted at almost every corner, but it was a nice excuse to spend some more time with Johann.

When they arrived in front of the *Wehrmachtheim*, Johann said, "Alexandra, it was a pleasure meeting you tonight. I wonder…would it be permissible if I were to seek you out in the coming days?"

"For what?" Lotte blushed, hoping the dim twilight of the summer night didn't give her away.

"I would like to get to know you better." His voice was soft, velvety even, as he perused her expression.

"I'm not sure that's a good idea, since we both have so much work to do," she answered.

"On the contrary, I think it's an excellent idea. Hard workers need time to relax, too." He raised the hand he held and kissed the back of her knuckles. "Will you allow me?"

"Yes." She couldn't help but agree.

He cast her a rare smile, one that struck a chord within her, and opened the heavy wooden door for her. "Goodnight, beautiful Alexandra."

CHAPTER 6

Berlin, July 1944

Peter spent so much time contemplating his next steps that he'd become a nervous wreck. Anna grew more worried about his lack of proper sleep by the day, and even his boss, Professor Scherer, had noticed and asked him several times whether he was alright.

It should have been a beautiful summer, a summer filled with hope as the Allies harassed the Wehrmacht from East and West, making their way across occupied Europe, freeing village after village from the vile grip of the Nazi oppressor.

Anna was delighted with the arrival of her niece Evelin, Ursula's daughter, but not even this happy event could make Peter smile. All he could think about was the fate of his compatriots and that he wasn't there to fight his share.

One day in late July while Peter was standing in the lecture hall with hundreds of uniformed medical students attending one of Professor Scherer's classes, a small, haggard man in his sixties approached him.

"Peter Wolf?" the man asked.

"Yes, who wants to know?" Peter looked at the balding man, who wore a cheap suit, mended many times.

"That doesn't matter."

Peter's neck hair stood on end and he scanned the room for possible exit routes. Had the Gestapo caught up to him? Unlikely, because this man didn't have the usual cocky attitude of a Gestapo thug. "What do you want?"

"I have a message for you. From Ewa."

"Ewa? I don't know any person by that name." Peter said, an icy chill coursing through his veins at the same time as he kept a calm façade. The only Ewa he knew was his former piano teacher in Warsaw, who now worked for the Home Army.

"Meet me at the Marienkirche in exactly two hours," the man said.

"How do I now you're legitimate?" Peter asked, but the man had already disappeared into the audience. Moments later applause for the Professor filled the hall, and Peter cursed the bad timing. With everyone leaving the lecture hall, his chances to follow the stranger were next to zero. Obviously, the man had planned it this way.

After driving the Professor to his lunch meeting, Peter asked for a few hours to run personal errands and set off to Alexanderplatz to meet the stranger. When he approached the church, a cold shiver ran down his spine. During a recent direct hit with incendiary bombs the church tower had collapsed onto the nave. The formerly beautiful

Marienkirche looked like an omen of even worse times to come.

Suddenly the aggravating feeling of running straight into a trap enveloped him like a cloak of trepidation. He glanced around, searching for someone who might have followed him. The risk was there, but if the man truly had a message from Ewa it must be important. She wouldn't contact him to exchange pleasantries.

He arrived at the same time the church bell struck two o'clock. The man from the lecture hall stepped out of the shadow of a building and stepped toward Peter, saying, "You came."

Off course I came, stupid! Or I wouldn't be here. "Yes."

"Let's go for a walk." Once they had left the crowded streets behind, the man said, "I'm Mariusz, by the way. And Ewa sends you this." He handed him a piece of paper with Ewa's distinctive handwriting. *There's great things about to happen. We need you at home.*

Peter squinted his eyes, still not fully convinced this was a legitimate message. "That doesn't say anything. And my home is here."

Mariusz switched to speaking Polish and said, "That's what you want everyone to believe, *Piotr*. But I know where your heart really belongs." With these words, he produced a red and white armband from his pocket. "This is the distinctive mark for all Home Army soldiers who will soon be fighting in the uprising against the Germans."

"An armband. You need more to convince me." Ripples of fear, but also of excitement, rushed through Peter's body. He'd been waiting for this opportunity for so long. But could he trust Mariusz?

"Poland needs you."

"Why now? Why not wait for the Red Army to liberate the country?" Peter asked, although he wasn't a friend of the Soviets. To him they were no less evil than the Nazis. The NKVD had proven to be even more efficient than the Gestapo in spreading terror, sending thousands of Poles to gulags in Siberia.

Mariusz sneered. "You're not really that stupid, are you? Haven't you heard what's happening? We fought alongside the Red Army to liberate Polish territory in the East, just to have the traitorous Soviets disarm, arrest or shoot our officers and forcibly conscript the lower ranks into their own army. Make no mistake, Stalin is out to conquer Poland, not free her."

"I agree. Stalin is a despicable dictator, on a par with his former old crony Hitler. But he's the ally of our allies, so he'll have to respect their wishes."

"And what makes you think they'll stay true to their word this time? They already sacrificed us on the altar of appeasing Hitler. They'll do the same for Stalin."

"True." Peter didn't have any response to that, since he'd never agreed on that point with the British and it still rankled that they'd let Poland down the first chance they got.

"It's now or never," Mariusz said. "The Soviet offensive crossed the old Polish border and our government-in-exile has to make a decision. We can either sit back waiting for the Soviets to roll their tanks across our soil, claiming the Home Army was a bunch of useless fools and collaborators. Or we can take our fate in our own hands and rise up against the Nazi oppressor. If we show the Western Allies that we played a crucial part in liberating our beloved fatherland, they won't let Stalin take her away from us again."

"I'll be there." Mariusz' heated speech had convinced Peter about his legitimate reasons. A spark of excitement had taken hold of him and in that very instant he'd formed the decision to fight for his nation. "When?"

"The sooner the better. We don't expect the uprising to last more than a few days, two weeks at most."

"Who will have instructions for me? You?"

"No. Travel to Warsaw and contact Ewa. She'll give you directions. General Bór is gathering the troops. And…bring a gun. We're a bit short on weapons."

"Thanks," Peter said, but his companion had already disappeared. *Damn, how can that man appear and disappear like a ghost?*

The rest of the day passed in a blur. After a very silent dinner, he asked Anna to join him in the sitting room. She snuggled up to him, tension oozing off her in waves.

"What's wrong?" she asked.

"Nothing." He paused, tugging a strand of her silky blond hair behind her ear. He hated how much he'd pain her with his plans. "I'm going back."

"Back? To where?" Her voice sounded alarmed and when she turned to look into his face, she blanched. "Don't tell me you're still thinking of going to Poland?"

Peter pulled a face. "Has it been that obvious?"

"Yes." Tears turned her eyes glassy, but she bravely held them back. "Tell me the whole story."

"I was contacted by a Home Army member today. They're planning an uprising against the Germans, and with the help of the Red Army, that's already chasing the Wehrmacht across Eastern Poland…it…I mean…my contact said it would be a matter of days or weeks."

Anna's paleness intensified, and he stopped talking, clasping her hands in his own. "Say something."

She looked at him and her voice trembled when she said, "I can't tell you I'm happy about what you've just told me, because I'm not. I'd rather have you here by my side…but I also understand. You were uprooted from your country, you lost your wife and son…I understand you need to be a part of taking Poland back." She gave him a sad smile and added, "I don't like the idea, but if that is what you need to do, I support your decision."

"Really?" He hadn't expected such a calm and mature answer.

"Really. Have you told London about this?"

"Not yet. Last time I mentioned the topic they wanted me to stay in Berlin. I might ask Professor Scherer for a few days off and travel to Warsaw. If my contact is right, I'll be back in no time at all."

Anna nodded, and he could tell she was both sad about him leaving and fearful that he might not return, but he also saw the strength in her eyes and her determination not to stand in his way. He loved her even more for that.

"When?" she asked after a lengthy pause.

"I'm going to ask him for the time off tomorrow."

"What excuse are you going to give?"

"I'm going to tell him I need some time off to take care of personal issues. Knowing Professor Scherer, he won't ask for more of an explanation than that."

"No, he probably won't. I will think about you while you are gone. Will you be able to write?"

"Probably not, since I am travelling under my real name." Peter raised one of her hands up and kissed her palm. "And I will think about you as well, but I'm not gone yet. What do you say I help you clean the dishes and we have an early night? I want to hold you in my arms."

Anna nodded and in the wee hours of the night, Peter awoke, Anna's head on his chest. He held her close as the sun rose, and he contemplated his next steps. With any luck, he'd be in Warsaw several days at most and when they'd chased the Nazis away he could return to his Anna.

Two days later Peter packed a small bag and waited for Anna to say goodbye.

"I love you," she murmured with bloodshot eyes testifying to her sleepless night.

"I love you too, sweetheart," he said and pressed her against his chest, inhaling her scent to commit it to memory. "Thanks for not trying to change my mind."

"Part of me understands why you have to do this, although the other part wants to tie you to the bedpost and keep you here with me," she said, trying to lighten the mood.

"That prospect will make me return in no time at all." He chuckled, sending her a dirty grin. He spent several moments admiring her embarrassed blush before he took her lips in a passionate kiss. "I love you."

"I love you, too. Promise you'll be careful and watch your back?" Anna handed him his hat, trying to hide her face, but he'd already spotted the treacherous shimmer in her eyes.

"You know I will."

"And if possible, please don't kill my sister Lotte." Her lips tugged upward but then fell again.

"Don't worry. As soon as fighting breaks out, the female auxiliaries will be immediately evacuated back to Germany. If the Nazis have gotten one thing right, it's protecting their women."

Anna cast him an angry stare and he held up his hands. "Hey, I hate them as much as you do, but in this issue they're right. They don't let women fight at the front like the Russians do. Female snipers. Fighter pilots. Soldiers. That's not what women were born to do."

"What about the British?" Anna asked, obviously trying to change the subject, since she was an advocate for equal rights, having fought tooth and nail to be admitted to medical university. Peter shared her opinion to some extent. Women should be allowed to vote, become scientists, doctors, train conductors, or whatever they wished…but there were limits. And without a shadow of a doubt, war was such a limit. A man's business.

He took a deep breath. "They don't know. I chose not to tell them."

"But what if something goes wrong?"

Peter pulled her into his arms and hugged her close, murmuring in her ear, "Nothing will go wrong."

Anna hugged him back, a shudder of emotion making her tremble in his arms. Knowing that the longer he delayed leaving, the harder saying goodbye would be, he squeezed her close one last time and then moved her back a foot. "I love you."

"I love you, too, Peter." Anna's eyes shimmered with unshed tears as she opened the door for him.

~

Peter disembarked from the train at the central station in Warsaw, taking a moment to calm his emotions. The city hadn't changed much in the past five years since he'd fled Poland after the invasion. It was amazingly wellpreserved compared to Berlin, which seemed to consist mostly of rubble and ruins nowadays.

In Berlin rarely a day, or more likely a night, went by without the unwelcome visit of the Allied bombers. On a rational level Peter understood that these bombings were a necessary evil in the grand scheme of the war, but emotionally, he couldn't fathom the amount of suffering the Allies inflicted on the civilian population.

He went to the address he'd committed to memory the day before and knocked on the door. It hadn't been possible for him to contact Ewa and tell her to expect him, but he knew she wouldn't turn him away and she'd have further instructions for him.

Light steps approached the door and a melodic voice asked in Polish, "Who is it? What do you want?"

"I was told you're giving adult piano lessons," Peter answered.

The door creaked open a crack and a thin woman in her forties with dark brown hair to her shoulders peeked out. "Who recommended you?"

"Mariusz."

She opened the door and let him inside.

"Thank you," Peter said after she bolted the front door behind him. "I am Piotr Zdanek."

Ewa's eyes widened and then she hugged him, kissing him on both cheeks, before she motioned for him to follow her. She settled at the piano and started playing a melody, murmuring in a low voice, "So you got the message. General Bór will be so pleased. He's been gathering the troops for the big thing."

"I'm here to fight for my country," Peter murmured in an equally low voice as he took a seat beside her and joined her playing the popular melody.

"You haven't forgotten your piano lessons," she said with a satisfied smile.

"I had the best teacher."

"Does London know?"

He shook his head, concentrating on his finger-play to keep up with her speed. It had been ages since he'd last touched a piano.

Ewa continued, "They haven't been very supportive of this endeavor. They're fearing diplomatic complications with our other neighbor…"

"I know," Peter answered, the conversation with Mariusz still fresh in his mind. Poland truly was located between a rock and a hard place. "You have orders for me? And a place to stay?" Ewa nodded and finished the song in silence, starting a new, more difficult tune.

"Very fitting," he murmured, glancing at the sheet music for *Spring* by Antonio Vivaldi, the Venetian master composer.

"The long winter is over. It's time to be out sowing the seed," she answered. "Go to Marek. He'll have a place for you to stay and he can take you to Bór." She gave him an address in the river suburb of Czerniaków and then said, "You need a nom de guerre. Don't divulge your real name to anyone."

He'd been living under a false name for more than two years, but the name Peter wouldn't sit well with his comrades, "Antonio."

"Vivaldi?" Ewa laughed. "Let's make it Antek."

He nodded as they finished Antonio Vivaldi's masterpiece.

"You must leave now, I'm expecting another student."

"Another student like me?" he asked with barely concealed curiosity in his voice.

"No, this one is German. She's on our side, but it would be best if you didn't see each other," Ewa explained.

Peter left her apartment, caught the tramway to the suburb of Czerniaków and thirty minutes later walked up the steps to an apartment building. He climbed to the third floor and knocked on the door.

"Who is it?" came a familiar voice from the inside. A voice he'd recognize out of a million.

"The long winter is over. It's time to be out sowing the seed." Peter used the code phrase Ewa had given him.

The door immediately opened, and a man waved him in, his lips pursing in displeasure when he recognized Peter. He looked Peter up and down, before he said, "So you've finally decided to come back and fight, coward?" Then he spat at Peter's feet.

"Thanks for the warm welcome, *Marek*." Peter doubted

whether he should stay here or seek a better place to sleep. Marek's real name was Jozef and the two of them used to be friends. They'd joined the army together and had fought side by side during the short weeks of the invasion. But when Peter had fled Poland with his unit to avoid spending the war in a German POW camp, Jozef had decided to stay and go underground.

"I thought I'd seen the last of your milquetoast face." His former friend stared at him with unconcealed hate.

"I'm here now, ready to fight."

"Did you have a good life in exile? Laughing every day about how your countrymen were tortured and slaughtered?"

"I didn't." Peter sighed. He'd not led a good life; he'd risked his life almost every day during these five years, first as a member of the British Expeditionary Forces and then as an SOE agent in Germany. But he chose not to mention this to his former friend.

"Since it looks like I'm stuck with you for today at least, you can bunk over there." Jozef pointed at the corner of the living room. "First thing in the morning we'll go and see Bór. Then he can decide what to do with someone like you."

CHAPTER 7

July brought insupportable heat to Warsaw, and Lotte spent her lunch hour in the Saxony Gardens, the small park adjacent to the German House, wishing she could get away from her work occasionally and dive into the cold waters of the Vistula River as she'd seen local boys do. It brought back pleasant memories of her childhood and especially her brother Richard. Of course, being a woman and an employee of the Wehrmacht made that notion out of the question; she could just imagine the pursed lips and raised eyebrows of Oberführerin Kaiser at such a crazy request.

"A penny for your thoughts," Johann's sonorous voice broke through her daydreams.

She jerked her head around. "I didn't hear you coming."

"May I sit down?" he asked, smiling at her.

"Sure." Lotte scooted down the bench to make space for him. It wouldn't be appropriate to sit next to each other so either one occupied one end of the bench.

"What were you thinking about? You had such a dreamy look on your pretty face."

"About my...home." Just in time Lotte caught herself before she said *brother*. Alexandra Wagner was an orphaned single child.

"I have those moments, too," Johann said, his eyes radiating his sadness. "But things are what they are, and we have to make the best of the present."

Lotte's stomach knotted every time she lied to him, and so she decided to offer him at least some tidbit of truth. "I saw the local boys swimming in the Vistula earlier and I dreamed of being able to do the same. Some cooling down in this oppressive heat would be delightful."

"You surprise me every day, Alexandra."

"Why?"

"Because...I didn't think you were one to swim in a river. You always look so prim in your uniform." He moved the slightest bit nearer, but still kept enough space between them in case of prying eyes.

"Oh. I was quite different when I was younger," Lotte said. *And you have no idea how different. I even had another name.* She glanced at her wristwatch. "I'm sorry. My lunch time is almost up."

"May I see you after work?" His light brown eyes lit up with hope and she hated to put a damper on them.

"I'd love to, but I have a piano lesson this evening," Lotte said, wanting to run a hand through her hair. After wearing it untamed and free all her life, she still hadn't fully gotten used to the braids that completed her new prim style.

"I could walk you there..." Johann suggested.

She feverishly debated how to decline his offer without

raising his suspicions and decided it would be most inconspicuous to agree. "That would be nice."

"At what time do you want me to meet you outside your office?"

"Would five p.m. work?" Lotte said, a genuine smile taking over her features. Try as she might, she couldn't rid herself of his charms, and every long day that passed, she looked forward to seeing him at the end of it. He was a bright spot in the midst of the mounting tension that seemed to sprawl across the entire city these days, infecting everyone and everything. On the surface, things in Warsaw were business as usual, but that sizzling tension was as real as the simmering heat that made it impossible to focus.

Punctual as the *Reichsbahn*, the German railway company, Johann arrived at her office in the evening and walked her over to Ewa's. Lotte talked like a chatterbox to hide her nerves, until he stopped and said, "Why are you so nervous?"

Lotte felt the tentacles of fear crawling about her skin. Great spy she was! "I'm...uhm...haven't you noticed the growing tension in the city? It makes me all jittery."

"So, you've been feeling it, too?" His brown eyes pierced deep inside her and she inwardly squirmed, fearing he could read her soul. Discover her true identity.

"Yes." She broke the mental connection. "The Oberführerin says we shouldn't worry, but at the same time she has us practice evacuation drills."

He seemed to be satisfied with that response, and they continued to walk until they stood in front of Ewa's apartment building.

"We're here," Lotte said, anxious to get rid of him. She needed to give Ewa the new codes for the week.

"Come out with me Friday night," Johann said, surprising her with the request.

"Out with you?" she parroted with a smile.

"Yes. On a date."

Lotte's smile froze in place and she averted her eyes, hoping she'd managed to hide the panic his words created. She liked Johann and part of her wished she were still as innocent and carefree as she'd been a year ago. But the scars ran deep, and he belonged to the very party responsible for it.

As she'd made a habit of doing since starting her new life, she took a moment to choose her words carefully. "Just the two of us?"

"Would that be so bad?"

She unconsciously bit her bottom lip, before daring to look at him. "I don't know...I would feel more comfortable..."

"...if we had other people with us?" Johann suggested softly, dipping his head to keep eye contact with her.

"Yes."

"Very well. I will ask Helmut to join us, with your room-mate. Would that be acceptable?"

Lotte felt such relief she gave him a big smile. "That would be perfect."

"At seven on Friday then? And do you own one of those swinging dresses?" he asked, and her heart skipped a beat at the implications of a swinging dress. Would he invite her out to dance?

"I will see what I can do. Until tomorrow," she said and

hastened into the safety of the building, away from the man who made her heart beat faster, or stopped it altogether, with one simple smile. She had no business being with him, or anyone else for that matter.

In Ewa's apartment, she played the piano with an unprecedented lightheartedness that her perceptive teacher immediately picked up on.

"Am I hearing love in your melody, Alexandra?" the older woman asked, and Lotte felt herself flush up to her hair roots.

"It must be the summer weather," she hastily said.

"The oppressive heat that has everyone nervous and moody makes you elated and floating?" Ewa cast her a knowing smile. At the very end of their lesson, the first one Lotte had truly enjoyed, Ewa said, "I don't want or need to know his name. I just want to urge you to be careful. Not everyone is who they seem, and if you're exposed it will have repercussions on many persons, including me."

Lotte looked at Ewa and answered, "I know this and that's exactly why nothing can develop between him and me. He's a Wehrmacht officer and if he knew..." She couldn't bring herself to finish the sentence.

"Take care." Ewa gave her a short hug and said almost apologetically, "I have quite come to like you."

"See you next week." Lotte rushed out of the apartment, fully aware that the relationship with Johann would lead her down a dangerous path. She helped the Allies to destroy the likes of him. She hated what he stood for. But she couldn't hate *him*. On the contrary—the more time she spent with him, the more likeable things she found.

In the dormitory, Gerlinde lay on her bed, reading a

book. She looked up as Lotte stepped into the room. "How was your piano lesson?"

"Wonderful. It actually sounded like music today and not just random noise."

Gerlinde laughed. "That was probably a welcome relief to your teacher's ears."

"No doubt. But I have more exciting news…"

"Let's hear!" Gerlinde sat up straight, her eyes beaming with curiosity.

"Johann asked me out…"

"That indeed is exciting news. It took him long enough," Gerlinde said with an infectious giggle.

"Well, I wasn't sure, so I asked him to make it a double date with you and Helmut. You don't mind, do you?" Lotte worried her lips with her teeth. Suddenly she had second thoughts about imposing on Gerlinde's private life.

Gerlinde rolled her eyes and gave a theatrical sigh. "I don't mind at all, but you really should have taken the opportunity to have him all for yourself. Anyhow, it'll be fun, and we can still separate later in the evening…" Gerlinde pushed forward, planning out the entire evening without stopping. "I've heard there's a singer scheduled for the troops and maybe even dancing. Did Johann mention dancing?"

"Not exactly, but he said something about a nice dress." Lotte flushed, thinking of the meager array of dresses she owned. Mentally going through her locker, she knew she possessed only one summer dress: an old-fashioned, bland green dress with a bright yellow pinafore. The pinafore was the only thing even remotely fashionable about that dress.

"That most certainly involves dancing then." Gerlinde

jumped up and rushed across the room to open her locker, taking out three different swinging summer dresses, each one more beautiful than the last.

Lotte's eyes turned wide as saucers when Gerlinde held up a spectacular pink dress. It boasted a sleek midriff with the skirt billowing out below, puffed-up short sleeves and white embroideries crisscrossing the waist, shoulders and skirt. But the dot on the i was the cute heart-shaped appliqué on the skirt with a pink bow and green beads dangling from it. The pink color perfectly matched Gerlinde's blonde hair.

"Absolutely gorgeous. You'll be the star of the night." Lotte considered the truth of her words. It wouldn't take much, because with her flirtatious smile and pretty face, Gerlinde always was the star with the men.

"What about you? Let me see what you're gonna wear."

When Lotte retrieved her green summer dress, Gerlinde's face fell. "No way in hell are you going to wear that! My own grandmother wouldn't be buried in that... thing...it's so last century."

"I don't have another one," Lotte whispered. The other girls had often teased her about wearing her uniform at all times. Truth be told, her clothing choices were extremely limited, and she couldn't compete with Gerlinde, Heidi and some of the other young ladies from wealthy families.

Gerlinde shook her head, as if she couldn't believe Lotte's words, before she took it on herself to scrutinize Lotte's locker. "You're right, there's nothing in there that's up to the occasion. I'll lend you one of mine."

"I can't possibly borrow one of your beautiful dresses," Lotte argued.

"Of course you can. You don't want me to walk alongside someone looking like the maid, now do you?" Gerlinde giggled and produced a beautiful cotton dress from the depths of her locker. "What about this? I never really liked it, because the color makes me look dull. But with your red hair, you'd be quite the doll. Try it on!"

Lotte did as requested and minutes later, she swirled in front of Gerlinde, Karin and Heidi, who'd just arrived at their room. The light grey cotton dress, printed with tiny flowers in white, yellow, red and blue, fit her like a glove. The simple v-neckline, short sleeves and a swinging skirt that ended just below the knees, made her feel sexier – and more mature – than ever before in her life. Just like Gerlinde had predicted, the pale grey, in combination with Lotte's red hair, made the dress an eye-catcher.

Heidi clapped her hands. "Gorgeous. Where are you going?"

"Alexandra secured us a double date with Helmut and Johann," Gerlinde said.

"The two dashing officers who came in from Lodz?" Karin asked, blatant admiration in her voice.

"Yes. The very ones. They're taking us to the dance in the soldiers' quarters." Gerlinde fiddled with the buttons on the dress Lotte wore.

"We're not sure there's dancing," Lotte said, slipping the dress over her head and feeling exposed in her underwear. She quickly slipped into her own clothes again.

"Yes, we do, because if there's no dancing at the garrison, we'll ask them to take us somewhere else. I do know quite a few places in Warsaw where they offer dance music on a weekend night."

Lotte could only shake her head. She'd never even thought about going dancing before today, but leave it to Gerlinde to have everything figured out in order to pass a jolly good time.

~

Friday evening arrived, and Lotte allowed Gerlinde's enthusiasm to infect her. After a considerable amount of discussion among the four roommates, it had been decided that Lotte would wear her hair down. Heidi helped tame the wild curls into stylish rolls using pin curls and sugar water.

Lotte slipped on Gerlinde's pretty dress and took a great amount of care with her make-up before she glanced at herself in the mirror.

"You're beautiful," Karin said, making last minute adjustments to Lotte's dress. "Johann won't know what hit him."

The urge to stick out her tongue became almost too great to ignore, but Lotte practiced a ladylike smile and nodded. Maybe going all out with her looks didn't serve her best interests? Johann might take it the wrong way and believe she was actually interested in him. Which she wasn't.

Shouldn't be.

Mustn't be.

"Come on; we're running late," Gerlinde said, grabbing her purse.

Johann and Helmut were already waiting outside the building to escort them, and Lotte felt Johann's appreciative glance on her person. Goosebumps broke out on her skin in the wake of his gaze. She could tell herself she wasn't interested all day long, but the truth was different.

"You look stunning, Alexandra," he said and offered her his arm.

"Thank you, you too." She inclined her head and gave him a shy smile. Both men wore their gala uniforms, and she swore there wasn't a better-looking man than Johann in all of the Reich.

They attended the concert and there was indeed some dancing to lively and upbeat music. Gerlinde, naturally, was a master at this new kind of dance, but after a while Lotte also got the hang of it and she had a fantastic time. Those moments of joy were so rare nowadays that she enjoyed them to the fullest and wished the evening would never end.

Gerlinde and Helmut disappeared from sight after Gerlinde had assured Lotte that she'd meet her in front of the dormitory by the time Oberführerin Kaiser expected them back.

"Let's take a walk along the river, before I return you home," Johann suggested some time later.

Lotte agreed, and they walked through the small park down to the river. She stopped to watch the rising moon's beams reflect over the water. "Isn't that beautiful?"

"It is. So peaceful…" he said, taking her hand, and they walked like that along the bank.

"I wish the war would end soon," Lotte murmured, deep in her thoughts.

"Who doesn't?" Johann squeezed her hand tight and stopped. "One day it'll be over and then we can all return home."

Lotte wanted to tell him that hundreds of thousands of

tortured, mistreated, starved and murdered people in the concentration camps couldn't return anywhere. And those who survived would have to live with the physical and psychological scars for the rest of their lives. But she couldn't well tell him this without blowing her cover.

It wasn't Johann's fault, either. Despite his obedience to the Nazi rules and ideology, he seemed to dislike the excessive amount of violence used, because she'd never seen him shout at, degrade or hit a Pole like so many other soldiers did.

"Where is your home?" she asked instead, knowing the danger of the topic, because he might dig into her past as well.

"I'm from Munich." He beamed with joy. "My parents have a small house in Schwabing, near the English Garden."

"The English Garden? Is it as big and beautiful as they say?"

"Even bigger and more beautiful," he said with a nostalgic chuckle. "Once the war is over I hope to be able to show you." His words caused her to panic and she jerked her hand from him, taking a step back.

"I'm sorry. I didn't mean to scare you."

"You didn't scare me. It's just…it's best not to make plans for the future." She swallowed. *Not because I don't believe in a future, but because you don't even know my real name.*

"I left my parents' house twelve years ago on the day I turned eighteen, to join the Wehrmacht. My parents disapproved, but I had big ideals. Well, that was in 1932 and the world was a different place. The first years were fun. I got to travel, even spent some time in Shanghai. When we invaded Poland, everyone thought this would be a fast and painless war. We go in. We win. The end. But look what has happened. It's five years later and we're still fighting. And every day more of my comrades get killed. We need peace and we need it fast." He glanced at her with eyes full of sadness, "I hate to say this, but I don't believe Germany can still win the war."

"You don't?" Lotte kept her voice steady, but inside, she all but screamed. Even the Wehrmacht didn't believe in winning anymore?

"Of course, I will fight as long as our Führer requires me to, but I wish the OKW would see what we see every day and negotiate with the Russians. They used to be our friends…"

Lotte rejoiced when they finally reached her dormitory, because this conversation could only lead to disaster. Maybe Ewa was right, and he'd been sent to sound her out. "We arrived. Thank you for inviting me out."

He stepped closer to her and enfolded both of her hands between his own. "It was my pleasure."

She felt the roughness of his hand, the calluses on his palms scratchy against her skin, and yet strangely comforting. This was not good. Not good at all. But it got worse… Johann stepped even closer, dipped his head, holding his lips just a breath away. "May I kiss you?"

Her breath stalled in her lungs, and she want to scream *No!* but instead she went up on her tiptoes and raised her chin to meet his lips with her own. The impact of his kiss made her legs give out and if he hadn't pressed a strong hand against her back, she'd have tumbled at his feet.

Lotte awkwardly moved back, placing several inches between them once again. "I should go."

"Have a good night, sweet Alexandra." Just at that moment a slightly disheveled Gerlinde whizzed around the corner with Helmut in tow.

"Thank God, I thought we were late," Gerlinde said and whispered into Lotte's ear, "You won't tell the Dragon anything, will you?"

"No. But let's go inside or we'll get into trouble." They walked up to the wooden door and then waved one last time at the two men standing in the moonlight.

CHAPTER 8

Johann walked back to his quarters in a very pensive mood. He'd thoroughly enjoyed the evening with Alexandra, but something had been trying to bubble up in his brain. Something he couldn't quite point his finger at.

He said goodnight to Helmut and then retreated to his quarters. One of the perks of his recent promotion to the rank of Feldwebel was a private room. Small, but all his. He slipped out of his gala uniform and hung it behind the door.

Alexandra's sweet face surrounded by the flaming red hair arranged in graceful rolls followed him as he prepared to go to sleep. It had been the first time she'd worn her hair loose and not in the – equally beautiful – plaits she wore at work. For some reason she'd looked so familiar this evening, as if he'd seen her before. But where?

He cast the thoughts aside. His mind was playing tricks on him. Lately he'd started to see familiar faces wherever he went. People on the street turned and he saw the face of a dead comrade. The more of his friends that perished in this dragged-out war, the more their ghosts seemed to haunt him when he looked at total strangers. He shrugged, not contemplating the implications.

Back in 1939 they'd been so enthusiastic, full of cocky assurance they'd win this battle in no time at all. And they had. Thanks to the OKW's brilliant *Blitzkrieg* strategy combined with the overwhelming superiority in trained men and materiel, the *Heeresgruppe Süd*, the Army Group South, overran the Polish Army in less than two weeks. After one month the Poland Campaign officially ended. The last Polish troops capitulated or escaped via Romania, dividing the country between the former friends Hitler and Stalin.

Everyone celebrated.

Everyone except the Poles.

Johann had believed the Poland Campaign necessary. After all, the shameful Versailles Treaty had stolen huge territories from Germany, both to the east and to the west. Germans accounted for about one third of the populace in the new Poland of 1919. This minority had the right to be relieved from the harassments of the Polish majority. So, yes, it had been a just cause to invade and take back what rightfully belonged to Germany.

But from then on, things spiked downward. Hitler didn't stop at taking back the lost territory; no, he invaded country after country to subdue to his Reich. At the beginning Johann had celebrated the fast victories together with everyone else, but slowly he'd questioned the reasoning.

The crusade wasn't about righting the sustained wrong anymore. It wasn't to restore the German honor. It had soon turned into a war of annihilation, with the declared goal to exterminate entire countries, nations or races.

Johann despised the amount of violence exercised against the civilians and had started to question the honorable motives when SS troopers rampaged through the occupied territories, leaving terror, death and destruction in their wake.

But by then it had been too late. With so many enemies left and right, the only way out of the mess was forward. Keep fighting – and hope for a better future after Hitler had occupied all of Europe and peace would prevail once more.

He finished brushing his teeth and sighed. Even if he wanted to, there was nothing he could do. In for a penny, in for a pound.

The next morning, his superior had a nasty surprise for the men.

Johann took an early lunch to seek out Alexandra in the mess. When he found her returning her empty tray, his heart leapt partly with joy and partly with sadness.

"Alexandra, can I talk to you for a minute?" he asked.

She turned and smiled at him, looking much older with her plaits and in uniform than last night in the stunning summer dress. "Shall we go for a walk?" she said over the noise of hundreds of people eating with clanging metalware.

They stepped out into the courtyard, bathed in glazing sunlight, and walked a few moments in silence, until they'd left the building behind and were headed for the river.

"The Red Army is approaching fast, and my unit will be deployed to reinforce the retreating *Heeresgruppe Mitte.*"

"What? Where? When?" she said with worry in her voice.

Johann shrugged, answering, "It depends. We'll leave the day after tomorrow. I go wherever the front line will be by then." Although, at the speed the Red Army smashed through German defenses, he might not have to go very far.

Alexandra shivered in the blazing sun.

"This was prone to happen." He tried to console her.

"I know, but it's a shock. Will you take care of yourself?" She took a step nearer and touched his hand for a fleeting moment.

"Always." They walked a few more minutes before Alexandra needed to return to her office. He wished he could seal the tragedy of the moment with a kiss, but with the owners of hundreds of prying eyes milling about, he chose to keep his distance. Liaisons between the female auxiliaries and the soldiers happened all the time, but they were not officially allowed or even encouraged.

"Will I see you to say good-bye?" she said as she turned to enter her office building.

"I cannot promise that, but I will do my very best to seek you out."

CHAPTER 9

Despite the unfriendly reception by his former friend Jozef, now called Marek, Peter didn't doubt for a single moment that he'd made the correct decision coming to Warsaw. Early in the morning, they visited the Home Army headquarters in the basement of a building in the Old Town.

About a dozen men in their forties filled the room, all veterans of the Polish Army who'd fought in 1939, judging by the uniforms they wore.

"Who's this?" A skinny man with a distinctive mustache and the insignia of a general asked Marek.

Marek introduced Peter. "He's Antek. Used to be in the Polish Army but fled to England after the invasion." The disapproval of Peter's actions was prominent in his voice.

"General Bór. I'm the commander of the Home Army," the man said and extended his hand.

"It's pleasure to meet you, General Bór," Peter said, careful to use the codename of the man he'd recognized as

Count Tadeusz Komorowski, a veteran from the Austro-Hungarian Army in the previous war.

"What's your rank?" a man asked, identifying himself as Colonel Mituk, Bór's right hand.

"*Podporucznik* in the Polish Army. After the invasion I joined the British Army and got later promoted from Second-Lieutenant to Captain."

"What's your battle experience?" Mituk asked, and Peter responded with detailed explanations about the short fighting during the invasion and his subsequent experiences with the BEF in France.

"Not bad, since we're in dire need of experienced men," another officer said.

Marek cast Peter a dark stare and murmured, "He's mostly experienced in running from danger." If Mituk heard the snide remark, he didn't reveal it, and instead proceeded to ask Peter questions about his whereabouts after the evacuation from Dunkirk.

"Did you bring a gun?" someone asked.

"A Mauser P08," Peter answered. Apparently, his contact in Berlin had been right and the Home Army was desperate for weapons.

"A P08? That's a fucking pistol! We're not going to win a war with a pistol," Marek said.

Mituk growled, "We have less than three thousand weapons to equip thirty thousand men. I'd take a P08 over nothing every day."

Marek drew his eyebrows together but gave a nod. Mituk turned to face Peter again saying, "Since you come recommended by two of ours and have battle experience, I'm awarding you the rank of Captain and assigning you to command the *Zoska* battalion. Radoslaw will show you." A murmur passed through the room, but nobody dared to oppose him, not even Marek.

"Come with me." A haggard man with the insignia of a Colonel, who must be Radoslaw, stepped forward. Peter later found out that Radoslaw was one of the main commanders in the uprising and his battalion was one of the best armed and best trained insurrectionist units.

"Good to have you on board. We need every able-bodied man to drive the Germans out," Radoslaw said. Since it wasn't safe to walk the street in uniform, he asked Peter to wait for him while he changed into civilian clothes.

Forty-five minutes later Peter stood in another basement, inspecting his *troops*—although they didn't deserve that name. Half of the *men* were below age, members of the Grey Ranks, the underground paramilitary Polish Scouting Association, and much to Peter's dismay, there were also a few women, or actually girls, among his troops.

"Have you ever had a weapon in your hands?" he asked them.

One fresh-faced boy with rosy cheeks raised his hand and explained, "We've practiced pulling apart, cleaning and putting back together several Russian, English and German weapons. We could do it wearing blindfolds."

"And we have learned everything about lobbing grenades and which way to throw them. Never upstairs," another equally young boy said.

"I see." Peter cast a desperate glance toward Radoslaw, who shrugged.

"How many of you have a gun?"

Nobody raised a hand.

"Any weapon?"

"I have my grandfather's hunting rifle," a slightly older boy admitted. "But the lever gets stuck most of the time."

"What about uniforms? Helmets? Boots?"

This time, a few hands rose. About a dozen of the men were veterans of the Polish Army and had kept their uniforms hidden throughout the occupation, while some of the younger boys had inherited pieces from fathers or older brothers.

"May I say something, sir?" a man with short black hair said.

"You may."

"We're planning to raid a shoe factory tomorrow morning, which should take care of the boots."

Peter forced himself to give a nod of approval. "Well, then. Await your orders."

On the way back to Home Army headquarters he didn't speak a word. Never in his life had he seen more badly trained and badly equipped troops. If this was the general state of the insurgents, they didn't have much hope of winning the uprising.

"What about the lack of weaponry?" he finally asked Radoslaw when they reached the headquarters.

"Very unfortunate. Most of the weaponry has been shipped to Eastern Poland in support of Operation Tempest. But we're confident we can capture enough German arms in the first day to equip three soldiers each to share one weapon." Peter shook his head, looking in Radoslaw's face for signs he was joking, but the other man was dead serious.

Later that same day, Peter met up with Colonel Mituk again.

"Have you inspected your battalion?" Mituk asked.

"Yes…but there's something I wanted to talk to you about. I'm concerned..."

"About?"

"Everything…" Peter said, doubt filling his voice. "They are untrained in regimented fighting, lack the basic weaponry needed to be effective, and I'm not sure how we can be expected to take on the Germans in this crippled state."

Mituk nodded his head and took a deep breath, before explaining, "I know all of this, believe me. But we simply cannot wait for better times. We have a very short window of time to secure Poland for ourselves, and that window will open soon. Once we start the surprise attack on the Germans, the fighting won't take long. Several days, a week at most."

"I don't see how that is possible. We're severely outgunned. Even with the element of surprise on our side…"

"We are not acting from a position of strength – nobody knows this better than I do – but we're in contact with London and Radio Moscow. In fact, we picked up a radio broadcast just today asking us to fight the Germans. The Red Army is approaching Warsaw with unprecedented speed, making good time day after day. As soon as we make our first strike to rid our beloved country of the Hitlerite vermin, they will come to our aid. Together we will win this battle."

A few other officers, including Marek, joined the discussion. "We should attack at the same time the Red Army does to maximize our advantage," someone said.

"No, they'll just claim the victory for themselves and take Warsaw out of our hands, the same way they've done with other towns."

"But we lose our advantage if we act too soon. We don't have the equipment necessary to mount a full-scale attack," Peter objected.

"So, you're saying we should hide?" Marek asked derisively. "You're very good at that, aren't you?"

Peter's anger at his former friend exploded, quick and fierce. "What are you implying?" He clenched his fists, tired of the innuendoes Marek constantly threw his way.

But before the situation could spiral out of control, an authoritative voice said, "The two of you need to stop this nonsense. Remember who the real enemy is and that you are on the same side. If we are to be successful, we must all work together."

Peter held Marek's gaze until the other man shook his head in disgust and walked away. When he turned to look at the rest of the group, he felt like he should say something to defend himself. He opened his mouth to do so, but one of the colonels stopped him with a gesture of his hand.

"Let the past go. We all made our choices. Neither way was better or worse. Marek is hurting, but he'll come around in time. As our commander said, we need every able-bodied fighter we can get. For Poland!"

"For Poland," Peter agreed, heeding the truth of the colonel's sage words. Now wasn't the time for petty quarrels. They had plenty of time for that after driving the Nazis out.

CHAPTER 10

Lotte returned to her workplace, trying to keep her focus on the radio transmission and not on Johann's imminent departure. But the content of the messages didn't help to dampen her fears. The Red Army seemed to have renewed their vigor; station after station sent frantic texts about being chased westward. Devastating losses led to a disorganized retreat, as the Soviets sent the Germans scrambling to figure out their next move.

While Lotte reveled in the imminent liberation of Poland, she also worried for the men dear to her heart. Her father had been a prisoner of war for so long, he probably didn't care either way, but as far as she knew, somewhere in Poland her dearest brother Richard was still alive and well with the Wehrmacht. The family hadn't heard from him in a few months, since he'd advised them that he'd chosen to leave his comparably safe post in a rear echelon and return to the front.

She could only wonder why he'd chosen to do so, but that didn't matter. Only his safety mattered. She scoffed. *Safety?* Deciphering the messages that came in, nobody in Poland was safe. Not even the *Wehrmachthelferinnen* in Warsaw. A shudder ran down her spine. She had no love for the Nazis, but the rumors surrounding the Red Army horrified her. In her position as a German woman, she preferred even the worst of the Nazi thugs to seeing a Soviet soldier eye to eye.

If Goebbels' propaganda was to be believed, and in this case she was inclined to do so, those sex-starved men knew no mercy and raped everything female. To them it didn't make a difference whether the woman in question was four, forty, or eighty years of age. And it certainly didn't matter to them whether their victim died of the violation or not. Lotte hunched her shoulders forward, wondering about her time in the concentration camp. Was that agony the worst a human could experience or was ratcheting up the suffering even possible?

No, it was best not to think about the rumors. If the Red Army succeeded in capturing the city of Warsaw and the women workers weren't evacuated on time, she would deal with whatever happened.

The next day, Oberführerin Kaiser ordered all the female helpers into the room they usually used for the folkloric events.

"Do you know what she wants?" Karin whispered.

"No idea, but it's very peculiar," Heidi answered.

The women gathered in the room, giggling and murmuring, until the Oberführerin arrived and motioned them to be quiet with one move of her hand.

"You will be asking yourselves why I have gathered this meeting," Oberführerin Kaiser began and looked around to see if everyone had arrived. "The Soviet Army is approaching Warsaw and our Führer in his immeasurable wisdom thought it prudent to start the evacuation sooner rather than later. All female personnel will be evacuated to their hometowns starting tomorrow morning. I'll put up lists in the hallway where you'll find the exact departure time of your train." It became so silent one could hear a pin drop. "Any questions?"

A petite girl with long brown hair and green eyes raised her hand. "What if your hometown is already in Russian hands?"

Oberführerin Kaiser raised an eyebrow. "We all know that this is only temporary, and the Wehrmacht will soon drive the Soviets from German soil again, but I agree it wouldn't be safe to send anyone eastward at the moment. How many of you have your homes in those territories?"

About two dozen women including Gerlinde and Heidi raised their hands.

"Well then, I will talk to the base commander about your case. Everyone pack your things and be ready for evacuation."

Everyone dispersed to their rooms to pack their belongings. Lotte wondered where they'd send her, since she had no hometown or family to return to in her identity as

Alexandra. She'd have to wait until the lists appeared in the hallway to find out.

"I don't want to go back to my boring little village," Gerlinde whined.

Lotte looked at her and shook her head. Despite being the youngest girl in the group, she felt like the grandma of them, always striving to be the voice of reason. "Boring is good. Boring means you are safe and away from the Russians."

"But there's nothing to do back home," Gerlinde wailed.

"You will survive. That is doing something," Lotte reminded her. "Besides, Helmut and Johann are leaving tomorrow as well."

Gerlinde brightened at the mention of her sweetheart. "Yes. Helmut has planned to take me out dancing tonight. One last evening of fun. Come with us?"

"Probably not. Johann already asked me to go for a walk with him later." Lotte grinned, placing the last of her belongings into the suitcase she'd arrived with.

"He likes you." Gerlinde giggled, doing a little silly dance.

"I like him as well." *And that's exactly the problem, because now I worry about him and his safety.*

Later that day, Oberführerin Kaiser hung the lists on noticeboards in the hallway and the female helpers gathered around, looking for their names and departure times. The group of women from the occupied territories found their names on a separate list, with the title *Evacuation pending until further notice.*

Lotte's name was nowhere to be found. She knocked on Oberführerin Kaiser's office.

"Herein!"

The Oberführerin sat at her desk, the phone receiver pressed to her ear, and motioned for Lotte to keep quiet and sit down. As far as Lotte could guess from the *yes, no* and *certainly, sir* answers, Oberführerin Kaiser was speaking to some superior.

When she finished her phone conversation, she glanced at Lotte, saying, "What is it? Are you packed?"

"Yes, ma'am. But I couldn't find my name on any list."

"That's not possible. Have you double checked?"

"I did. Three times."

Oberführerin Kaiser took out her own set of lists, sorted by administrative region. "Where are you from?"

"Well, I enlisted and took my basic training in Cologne."

"Not where you enlisted. Where your family lives," the Oberführerin said, while running her finger down the list for Cologne.

"I don't have family anymore," Lotte answered.

The older woman looked up for a moment, seemingly surprised, but her voice didn't show any trace of emotion as she said, "Where was your last registered place of residence?"

That would be the concentration camp in Ravensbrück. "I lived in an orphanage with nuns near Munich, but I had to leave that place when I turned eighteen. The good women won't be able to take me back; they have enough children who need their care more than I do."

Frau Kaiser's long and slim finger trailed down the lists for Munich, Berlin, and all the other scheduled trains, but the name of Alexandra Wagner was nowhere to be found. After a while she raised her voice again saying, "It seems you're not on any train, because you weren't registered in any of the administrative regions in Germany. I have no idea how this could happen. You'll join the group of girls from the occupied territories and wait for further orders."

"Yes, Frau Oberführerin. Thank you," Lotte said, getting up to leave the office.

"The Führer will not abandon you. I'll make sure you and the other *Helferinnen* are evacuated to a safe place in Germany."

Lotte doubted the truth of her words. From the way things were going, soon there wouldn't be a safe retreat anywhere on the continent, and she could only hope not to fall into the hands of the vile Russians. From everything she'd heard whispered behind closed doors, it was by far preferable to fall into the hands of the Americans or English. Frenchmen seemed to take a middle ground on the scale of cruelty against German women but were still preferable to the Russians.

Johann picked her up after work and took her out for dinner in one of the fancier restaurants that were reserved for officers.

"I heard the female employees are being evacuated. When are you leaving?" he asked, taking her hand.

"I don't know yet."

"How come?"

"Since they don't know where to return me, I'll be waiting here with the girls from Eastern Poland for further orders."

"Oh yes, we cannot send them into the territories that are already under Russian occupation. But why you?" His tone was full of concern.

"Before joining up, I lived with nuns in an orphanage." Lotte repeated her cover story, secretly longing to tell him the truth. She hated lying, and before changing her identity and becoming a spy, she'd never considered how much the constant lying, cheating and faking would bother her. What kind of courtship was this, where she couldn't even trust her man with her real name? She shook her head and cast her eyes downward murmuring, "Let's talk about something else, please."

"What would you like to talk about?" he asked.

"Music?" Music was innocuous.

"Helmut and some of the others have taken their girls dancing. Would you like to go, too?"

"No, I'm not in the mood for celebrating. I'd rather spend our last evening talking," she said and by the shine in his warm brown eyes he shared her preference.

"Come for a walk with me along the river," Johann said and asked the waiter for the bill. They walked through the park down to the riverbank, where many other couples lingered in the warm evening, the sun slowly sinking behind the horizon and casting the water in a pink and orange glow. In the distance they heard the constant sound of mortar fire, like the drums to a piece of music.

"The Red Army is approaching," Lotte said.

"Yes, but there's no need to worry. They won't be able to cross the Vistula. We have reinforced all the bridgeheads with extra guards."

That was very valuable information and Lotte suddenly

remembered Ewa. "May we stop by my piano teacher's house? I know it's late, but I feel like I should leave her a note, letting her know I won't be returning and to thank her for everything she's done for me."

"We can walk that way."

Lotte walked through the city streets with Johann holding her hand. An eerie silence cloaked the streets. Poles weren't allowed outside after curfew, but usually any number of groups of soldiers and female auxiliaries could be found milling about.

They reached Ewa's building and Lotte walked up to the third floor to slip a note beneath the door. Then Johann delivered her back to the dormitory.

"I guess this is goodbye – for now," he said quietly, looking into her eyes.

She nodded and then on impulse, she hugged him. "Be careful."

"I will. I want to see you again." He tried a chuckle, but it sounded more like a snort.

He kissed her on the lips and then handed her a piece of paper with a number on it. "Here's my *Feldpostnummer*. Will you write me?" The *Feldpostnummer* was an identification number used for military mail service. Even without knowing a soldier's location, his family and friends could still send letters and parcels to his unique number.

"I should go inside," she whispered. If this parting became any more emotional, she might blurt out her true identity so he would have a chance to find her after the war.

"I should go as well. We leave at first light."

Lotte hugged him one last time and fled inside before he could say anything else. Her roommates hadn't returned yet and she wrote a letter to Anna, letting her *best friend* know about the evacuation and that she would contact her again when she knew her final destination.

She stared at the four suitcases neatly stacked besides the door. Another chapter of her life would soon be closed.

CHAPTER 11

Peter had been diligently training the *soldiers* under his command. They were eager and willing, but he couldn't make up for a lack of proper military training in a matter of days. If only he had arms for each one of his men, but for now they had to make do with ten men sharing one weapon.

On July 31st of 1944 General Bór called for a meeting with all his officers. Peter and Marek arrived at the head-quarters with time to spare, but when they stepped into the room, they realized everyone else was already there.

"Sorry for being late," Peter said.

"You're not late, since everyone else was early. But let's not waste more time," General Bór's confidante Colonel Mituk said and waved them forward.

Bór laid out a map of the capital on the large wooden table and began to explain his plan. "The time has come. I am ordering the full mobilization of all forces."

The tension in the room exploded as everyone snapped

to attention, devouring the instructions of Mituk, who now took over the explanations. "W-Hour is tomorrow, August 1st, at 1700 hours." He pointed at several officers and then put his finger on the designated concentration points on the large map, explaining, "You take your units to Zoliborz, the Old Town and the City Center. It's important to have our entire troops mobilized and gathered in the designated buildings. Weapons will be distributed as we obtain them."

The officers nodded their heads, gathering closer around the table to find the buildings where they had to wait for *wybuch*, the Polish word for outbreak.

"I don't have to remind you how important the element of surprise is. Under no circumstances must the Germans get wind of our plans."

After several minutes of discussion, Marek raised his voice. "What about uniforms?"

"Naturally, everyone who owns a uniform will wear it. Everyone else has to make do with what he has," Mituk explained.

Peter grimaced. An army without weapons, and without uniforms. That wouldn't be well received under the Geneva Convention. "But wouldn't that make us partisans that the Germans don't have to treat like enemy soldiers, but can do with as they please?"

"Unfortunately, yes. But there's no way we can organize uniforms. Those who own one from previous battles are the lucky ones; the rest better not get caught," Mituk said with a grin, trying to lighten the mood. Everyone in the room knew what the Nazis did with the insurgents whom they called *Banditen*.

"How will we distinguish fighting insurgents from civilians?" Peter asked.

Colonel Mituk waved a young man with a heavy sack forward. He opened the sack and took out red and white armbands. "Everyone who wears this is a soldier of the Home Army. Take armbands for all your men, and some to spare. This is one of the few plentiful things we have."

Ten minutes later Peter and Marek left the headquarters and returned to Marek's place to gather their uniforms and start the telephone chain to inform their troops, so everyone would arrive at the concentration points before nightfall. Peter thought of his sister-in-law Lotte and hoped she'd long left Warsaw. After tomorrow nobody would be safe in this city anymore.

"Wouldn't it be better to surprise the Germans in the morning? Our men aren't trained soldiers and would do better fighting in the daylight," Peter said, more to himself than otherwise as he checked on his Mauser pistol. Since it was a German pistol, he was confident he'd find ammunition for it somewhere should the uprising last more than a few days.

"Trying to back out already?" Marek said in a snide tone. "The Nazis hate fighting at night, so they won't expect us to begin a battle in the evening. And the cover of darkness will give us an advantage. We know our city a lot better than they do...except for people who chose to spend the last five years far away."

"That's enough!" Peter replied. On the eve of the uprising, it was high time to put their differences aside. "Jozef, it's obvious..."

"It's Marek." Marek looked him dead in the eye.

"Well, then. Marek. It's obvious you have a problem with me. And it's equally obvious that your animosity towards me will not help us win this battle. So, let's get it out of the way once and for all. What's your problem?" Peter stood in front of his former friend, feet planted hip-width apart. If Jozef needed a brawl to get over his animosity, he wouldn't shy away.

"I'll tell you what my problem is, asshole. You cannot be trusted." Marek spat on the ground.

"What makes you think so? When have I ever done anything to deserve this accusation?"

"You abandoned your country. You took the easy way out and fled when the Nazis came and crushed us. Do you have any idea how hard it was to live five years under their occupation?" Marek's loud voice shook with emotion.

"You think I had it easy? That you were the only one to suffer? You know nothing." Peter took a step toward Marek, staring him down.

"Don't I? Explain it to me then. Tell me how your fleeing to Britain was so hard." Marek stepped forward until their foreheads were mere inches apart.

"The Brits and the French promised to stay by our side should Hitler invade, and I believed them. I…we all… strongly believed they would keep their promise and attack. It was only natural to evade capture and join the British Army. The idea was to return and liberate Poland."

"That went quite well, did it?" Marek sneered.

"You're right; it didn't work out. After months of prepa- ration, the Wehrmacht vanquished us in France and we were lucky enough to get out of Dunkirk. If Hitler had annihilated the BEF right there and then, there wouldn't have been a sliver of hope left for a free Europe."

"Oh, now you're the savior of free Europe and not the coward you effectively are?" Marek glared at him and Peter almost surrendered to the overwhelming urge to retreat. But he wouldn't budge.

"I'm not a coward. You have no idea how many of my men I saw die. And don't you think I would have preferred to be here when my Ludmila and Janusz were taken to the Ghetto in Lodz? Don't you think I would have wanted to be with them and find a way to rescue them? Don't you think it was hard to get the notice they were both killed?"

Marek didn't waver from his point of view. "You're right. You should have been here, but instead you lived a peaceful and comfortable life in Berlin and became subservient to the German pigs. I know all about you and your Nazi professor. Driving a Mercedes for a piece of shit, what a heroic task to help Poland!"

"You're even more of a dumbass than I thought. You really think it was easy holding my tongue and saying nothing when those Nazi pigs started running their mouths? You think it was easy having to stand by and watch one atrocity after another and not being able to do anything to stop it?"

"Maybe you should have done *something*. At least you'd die a righteous man and not a filthy collaborator," Marek said.

"I'm not a collaborator! How dare you?" Peter balled his hands into fists, fighting the urge to strangle the stubborn man who insisted on baiting him with his dirty insults.

"Well…that's what we call it around here, when you

make your bed with the occupiers. And people get executed for that. I honestly have no idea why Bór accepted you as a fighter…why he even gave you a battalion."

Peter stared at his former friend, still not fully believing that Marek had called him a collaborator. Instead of setting them to fighting shoulder to shoulder for their country, this atrocious war had made enemies out of friends. "Look, man. I came here with one goal in mind. Destroying the Nazis."

"Well, at least we still have that in common," Marek murmured beneath his breath.

"W-Hour is tomorrow. I'd feel a lot more confident if I knew you had my back, instead of having to fear you'll feed me to the lions the moment you get a chance," Peter said.

"Turn you in to the Nazis? I'd never stoop that low. I'd rather kill you myself."

"If that isn't a relief," Peter answered with a sarcastic smile. "Truce?"

Marek looked at his outstretched hand and grudgingly shook it. "Fine. Truce. For Poland. But only while the operation lasts. I'm going to bed."

Peter watched him disappear into his bedroom and then he quietly prepared himself something to eat, thinking about his beloved Anna. He yearned to send her a letter, but that wasn't possible. Since he'd slipped back into his Polish identity, he had no business contacting her. A simple letter from him might cause the Gestapo to ask uncomfortable questions.

He could only hope and pray for her continued safety, despite the constant allied air raids on the city of Berlin.

CHAPTER 12

August 1, 1944

L otte awoke the next morning tired and wishing she could hide beneath the covers. Throughout the day, most of her colleagues would board the trains back home. While she didn't want to join them, she felt nostalgic for her newfound friends now that they wouldn't be around anymore.

At least Gerlinde and Heidi would stay until someone higher up the chain of command figured out where to send them.

"Aren't you going to breakfast?" Gerlinde asked moments later.

"I don't feel much like eating this morning. I'm already missing the others." Lotte put her head between her hands.

"Come on, there's no reason to mope. And we still have to go to work today," Heidi said.

"You're right. At least the two of you are staying here." It was entirely selfish to think that way, but Lotte couldn't help it.

"Are you ready? I'm hungry," Gerlinde complained impatiently.

"One minute," Lotte said and slipped on her uniform, making sure the garrison cap sat fashionably crooked on her braided hair. While all the other girls adored the uniform, Lotte had a more difficult relationship with it. She loved how it made her look mature and earned her the respect of her male colleagues, but she also hated what it represented. Every day she reminded herself that she was in Warsaw to bring down the Nazis and not to join in their jolly celebrations.

The problem was that everybody was so nice, even Oberführerin Kaiser. In Ravensbrück it had been easy to hate the cruel *Aufseherinnnen* with their batons and lashes, but here? How could she hate someone like Gerlinde and Heidi? Helmut? Johann? She couldn't even hate her superior, Oberst Braun. He'd never been anything but friendly and fair to her and the other female employees. He was simply doing his job, obeying orders like everyone else.

Lotte gave a deep sigh, her head throbbing as she tried to resolve the issues of hate, guilt and responsibility. It wasn't that easy. Nothing was. She couldn't risk hurting other people again with her rash decisions. The guilt of being responsible for the death of two dear friends, whose only crime had been to help her, still weighed heavily on her shoulders.

"You coming, or what?" Gerlinde's voice dragged her from her philosophical thoughts.

"Yes." Together they walked the ten minutes to the mess, the room perceptibly emptier than usual. But much to her surprise, she spotted Johann at his usual table and walked over.

"Good morning. I thought you'd be gone by now," Lotte said.

He answered her with a broad smile. "Change of plans. OKW has given the order to defend *Fortress Warsaw* at all costs. We'll stay in the city and counterattack the Red Army as soon as they reach the eastern shore of the Vistula. The river and the bridgeheads will give us a natural advantage. What about you?"

"No news yet. Most of the other girls are boarding the different trains as we speak. I expect the rest of us will receive orders tonight."

"I know this is selfish, but I'm glad you're still here. You brightened my day." Lotte blushed at his compliment and murmured something about having to go sit with Gerlinde and Heidi, before she dashed off. Her feelings for Johann were confusing at best. On the one hand she longed to show him how much she liked being with him, while on the other hand she wanted to keep him at arm's length.

Throughout the day, Lotte felt torn between wanting to stay in Warsaw to do her bit and wanting to flee. The sound of heavy mortar fire and gunshots seemed to come nearer by the hour and trails of smoke rose in the sky just beyond the city. No doubt the Russians were near. Almost close enough to see them across the Vistula. Chills rolled down her spine and froze the blood in her veins at the prospect of what might await her should the Russians capture her – in uniform no less.

Shortly before five o'clock that evening, she finished her work and met with Gerlinde to walk to the dormitory and see whether they'd been assigned an evacuation train yet. They'd walked about one block, when suddenly the world seemed to explode around her. Lotte felt as if someone had thrust her into the heart of a battle scene in a movie.

But this wasn't a movie.

The street suddenly filled with Polish insurgents, mostly in civilian clothes, wearing red and white armbands. Some fired their weapons, others lobbed grenades, but all of them moved toward the town's key strategic buildings.

With great presence of mind Lotte grabbed Gerlinde's hand and dragged her bedazzled friend back towards their office building. Alarms sounded, adding to the deafening noise. She honestly had no idea how they made it the one block into the safety of the *Oberfeldkommandantur* without being injured. From what she could see, the entire Old Town and City Center districts were one huge fireball.

The inside of the military building resembled a beehive. Hundreds of surprised Wehrmacht soldiers milled about, waiting for their orders. More than once Lotte and Gerlinde had to press against the wall to evade being trampled down by a group of soldiers rushing to fight the insurgents.

Something hit the building and the smell of burned human flesh attacked Lotte's nostrils, making her gag as it brought memories of her time in Ravensbrück. She'd never forget this smell for the rest of her life.

"Let's go and see what we can do," Lotte said, dragging a whimpering Gerlinde behind her to the radio operations room upstairs. Since most of the radio operator girls had left Warsaw throughout the day, only one of the desks was occupied. A girl called Sandra tried to decipher the cacophony of transmissions.

Oberst Braun entered the room, his expression a mask of shock and disbelief at the events outside. "Thank God, you're here. I need you to work through the phone calls and radio transmissions to get a picture of the situation. Give me a status report in fifteen minutes." As quickly as he'd entered the room, he disappeared again, leaving the three girls on their own.

"Let's get to work then." Lotte sat down at her usual desk, ignoring the constant ringing of the dozens of phones in the room. She put on her headset and concentrated on deciphering the messages coming in from stations across the entire city at a feverish pace.

When Oberst Braun returned, the three radio operators had a much clearer picture and he confirmed their suspicions. This wasn't an isolated attack on some of the German military buildings, but a carefully planned concerted action. An uprising. Lotte's heart beat faster. The Poles actually had the nerve to take fate in their own hands and fight against their oppressor. And it looked like they held all the aces.

Every minute more bad news arrived. Significant areas of Warsaw's left bank districts had been captured by the insurgents, including the prestigious Prudential high-rise building, the main post office, and the state mint. Several officers poured in and out of the radio room, wanting updates on the situation. Lotte, Gerlinde and Sandra did their best to keep up with the influx of messages, jotting down the crucial information.

The next message came in: *East-west railroads severed*

Lotte had to lean back and remind herself to breathe. She could only hope that her evacuated colleagues had made it out safely before the tracks had been blown up. Her entire body shivered violently when she became aware that she and Gerlinde were trapped inside the most violent revolt since the beginning of the war.

"What's wrong, Alexandra?" Gerlinde asked, worry lines etched on her face.

"No…no…nothing."

"Lean back for a moment, I'll get you some water," Gerlinde said and dashed off. Usually food and drink were strictly forbidden in the radio room because they could damage the expensive equipment, but today nobody cared. Lotte glanced at the clock on the wall. It was way past midnight. There was no way they could get back to the dormitory even if they wanted to.

Minutes later Gerlinde returned with a glass of water and some bread. "Here. This will help. Are you sure you're feeling well?"

Lotte nodded. *No, I'm not. Any moment the insurgents can burst through the door and kill us all.* Given the way the Germans had treated the Poles for so many years, Lotte didn't have much hope of being treated with decency should she fall into their hands.

"Thanks," Lotte whispered after eating the piece of bread. "I guess I can get back to work now." She ignored her exhaustion and continued to sit hunched over her desk, deciphering message after message.

Sometime in the wee hours of the morning, Johann staggered into the radio operations room for a brief moment. He looked exhausted, smears of dirt, grease and dust on his uniform, and he sported a bloody wound above his right eye.

"You're injured, let me—"

"It's nothing. Merely a scratch," he answered. "How's everything in here?"

"Stressful but safe for now."

He wiped his sleeve across the wound on his forehead and flinched for a moment. "You should have been evacuated by now. The Wehrmacht doesn't allow female helpers in battle zones."

Lotte gave a dry laugh. "All east-west arteries have been severed. There's no way out of this city at the moment."

"I should have insisted they send you out on one of the trains this morning." Suddenly, he looked very tired.

"Oberst Braun says it's a matter of days until we regain the upper hand," Lotte said.

"That's what everyone's saying. But those *Banditen* are fighting like maniacs. They have self-made grenades, flamethrowers in bottles and apparently had an underground factory producing firearms, directly under our noses." Johann shook his head. "Who would believe they could pull off an organized uprising like this one?"

Lotte smiled at him and quarreling emotions created a lump in her throat. She wanted Johann to be safe, but at the same time she wanted the Poles to win this revolt and send the Nazis to hell. Since when had life become so complicated? Even last year everything was black and white for her. Good and evil, neatly separated from each other. But life as an adult didn't seem to work that way. It was a hellish muddled mess painted shades of grey.

"Tired?" Johann asked and traced a finger down her

cheek. She nodded automatically and flushed furiously when he cupped her jawline and kissed her with unprecedented passion, not caring that one of the superiors could burst into the room any moment. "Promise me you'll stay in here? This building is our number one priority to defend against the insurgents."

"I will. Promise me you'll be careful out there?"

"I don't have any intentions of dying this young. Besides, I have you to come back to," Johann said, kissing her again before standing up and disappearing into the midst of the battle-strewn city.

Lotte refused to let her tears fall and returned to work until around six in the morning. Oberführerin Kaiser arrived with the remaining dozen *Helferinnen*. Apparently, they'd escaped minutes before the Home Army had stormed the dormitory. The Oberführerin was happy to find the missing three girls safe and sound and ordered them to go to the basement and get some sleep in a makeshift dormitory.

When Lotte emerged from the basement many hours later, she glanced out of the window into the blazing sun. The amount of destruction visible sent a queasy feeling to her stomach. Most of the buildings in the Old Town stood in flames, clouds of smoke hanging low in the sky. She later learned that most of the Old Town and the City Center were in the hands of the insurgents, except for the headquarters of the German garrison, and the bridges over the Vistula.

They were basically trapped inside the building, unable to venture out into enemy territory. Even chatterbox

Gerlinde grasped the ugly reality and kept her mouth shut for the first time since Lotte had met her months ago. Soldiers moved in and out of the building, mostly to bring in wounded comrades or replenish ammunition reserves. Lotte hoped to see Johann again, but no such luck.

CHAPTER 13

Peter had spent the past few days in a constant cycle of fear and euphoria. Since the Germans hadn't suspected any kind of organized resistance, they'd been utterly unprepared, and the Home Army captured significant areas of the city. By the end of day two, gas, electricity and water were securely in Polish hands.

The Germans concentrated their forces on defending military installations and important communication infrastructure like the telephone exchange, the central train station and the airport.

"We have to build barricades against their tanks," Peter ordered his men late at night.

"But how?" someone asked and gestured to the scene of destruction on the streets in the Wola district.

"The tramcars," a young blond boy suggested and pointed his finger down the street.

Peter glanced in the direction and saw an abandoned

tram standing on the tracks, half of the tramcars derailed. "It's worth a try," he said.

With twenty men they managed to put the derailed cars upright and pushed them along the tracks past the next crossing.

"Here. Put two tramcars at a right angle to the street and push the other ones further down around the corner." It was tough work and despite the light evening breeze, sweat poured down Peter's back. Soon enough other units followed their example and by nightfall they'd managed to build an intricate network of street barricades, preventing the Germans from having easy access despite their Panzers.

While the German garrison seemed to be on a par with the Home Army in numbers of soldiers, it was greatly superior in arms, tanks and ammunition. Peter always had to remind his men not to shoot if it wasn't absolutely necessary, or they'd run out of ammunition before the fighting ended.

That night, they retreated into the upper floors of a nearby building, getting some much-needed sleep. Peter placed guards at the entrance and the windows, but he needn't have worried. The Germans, who loathed night-fighting, seemed to have gone to sleep as well.

The next morning, a young boy with the red and white armband passed the manned barricade, bringing them copies of the first issue of the *Biuletyn Informacyjny*, the Information Bulletin newspaper. It contained four pages with the most important news and was distributed free of charge by a network of messengers – boys too young to be allowed to fight.

Later that day Peter received orders to move his

battalion further south to capture a large Waffen-SS warehouse with food and military uniforms. He grinned at the command. Food wasn't an issue, but his men would love to get their hands on real uniforms. Most of them still wore civilian clothes, some even shorts and sandals, as the mobilization had surprised them while out and about.

The SS had abandoned the warehouse as Peter's battalion reached it, leaving only one of their comrades behind, who'd barricaded himself inside the building. It didn't take long until the young SS trooper was shot, and Peter's men raided the warehouse.

Half an hour later, Peter inspected his troops and chuckled. Everyone wore proper boots, helmets and leopard-spotted camouflage smocks, called *panterka*, graciously provided by the Waffen-SS. They weren't in accordance with the rules of war, but how could he deny his men the pleasure of wearing a uniform, and one of the most coveted modern camouflage tunics on top?

He sent a messenger to headquarters about the capture of food and ammunition and secured the weapon of the dead SS man.

"Who knows how to fire a Schmeisser?" he asked his men.

One boy stepped forward. "I do."

Peter had his doubts whether the boy had actually fired a gun before, but he still handed it over. "Take good care and only fire in short bursts when absolutely necessary."

The boy nodded with a self-important expression on his face, and Peter mentally counted his men and the arms he had for them. Fifty-seven fighters and seven firearms. He'd prefer to find weapons over uniforms any day.

"We'll take a break. Eat and rest." He gave his men orders, organized guards and took two of the more experienced soldiers outside. From the direction of the river they heard the explosion of mortar bombs and heavy machine guns.

"Probably the Red Army on the other bank. When will they cross?" a man called Radwan said.

"Soon, I hope." Peter had no idea what was delaying the Red Army. They'd been camping on the other side of the Vistula for almost a week. Why didn't those damn Russians just cross and relieve the Polish resistance?

"There's bad news from the Zoliborz area," the other man, called Niedzi, said. A courier had brought news of the Zoliborz battalion running into truckloads of SS troopers and several Panzers, coming to the aid of their Luftwaffe friends, who'd been caught unawares by the insurgents. After suffering severe casualties about half of the battalion had managed to escape into the nearby forest.

"At least they can replenish their ammo with the partisans out there," Radwan said.

"Why don't the British drop supplies for us?" Niedzi asked.

Peter had asked himself the same question. "I guess they do, just not inside the city, because the probability of dropping into the German area is too great."

The battalion returned to their position of the previous night and occupied the upper floors of one of the buildings. In the late afternoon someone shouted an alarm as a bunch of Wehrmacht soldiers stormed the barricades. Heavy fighting ensued, and Peter's unit had to retreat into one of the buildings.

Years ago, the Germans had required holes be drilled into the basement walls to interlink the houses for easier access. This proved now to be very useful as the Poles escaped through the basements into an empty building, where they moved to the upper floors and positioned guards at the staircase. Soon enough they heard heavy footsteps and shots. Peter motioned for everyone to be quiet.

"Hände hoch, Banditen!" That was the order to put up their hands and surrender. Nobody moved, because they knew all too well what happened to captured *Banditen*. About a minute later the Germans shot with their Schmeissers, hoping to penetrate the floorboards of the upper rooms. The heavy footsteps roamed about and finally became more distant.

"They're gone," someone whispered.

"I'll check." Peter took two of his armed men downstairs and searched the building. Empty. He leaned against the doorjamb for a moment, pondering whether they should stay here for the night or not, when someone barreled into him from behind.

Peter tumbled to the ground, as a burly Wehrmacht soldier wrestled the weapon from his hand and came to sit astride him, pointing the muzzle of the handgun directly at his head. Peter was sure he'd seen his last day on this earth when the report of a gun being discharged echoed in his ears and the German fell sideways, a gaping hole in his forehead.

He scrambled to his feet to see a very pale boy crouched in the doorway, slightly trembling, but holding his newly acquired Schmeisser at the ready to fire again if needed.

"Nice shot, thank you," Peter said, picking up his own

gun from the floor and securing the German's weapon as booty to arm yet another one of his men. "Let's finish clearing the building."

They scared the returning enemy soldiers away by lobbing self-made grenades at them and then gathered upstairs with the rest of their unit to eat some of the rations they'd taken from the raided warehouse.

Everyone else was already asleep when Peter checked on the guards again. Communications had been almost nonexistent, and he was in dire need of new orders. The next morning he'd have to go to headquarters himself to find out about the bigger picture.

But it took almost two days before the skirmishes with the enemy finally allowed him to leave his position and make his way to Bór's headquarters. A few of the officers, including Marek, were discussing the overall situation when he entered the room. Marek greeted him with an ice-cold stare but kept his usual animosities to himself.

"The majority of the city is now in our hands, and the Germans have retreated into their bunker-like strategic buildings, waiting for reinforcements," Colonel Mituk said.

"What the hell are the Russians waiting for? We need them to attack before the German reinforcements arrive." Marek's words only echoed everyone's thoughts. Hadn't Radio Moscow promised to fight side-by-side with the Poles in case of an uprising?

"They stall," another colonel with the codename Romek said and spat on the ground. "Who knows what Stalin is planning? He's not one whit better than Hitler. Have you all forgotten what *he* did to Poland? How come he's now supposed to be our savior?"

"Because he's the ally of our allies. He won't dare occupy our country again. The British will see to it," Mituk answered.

"The British? What have they done so far? Nothing," Marek said.

"Yes, they should fly in the Polish parachute brigade. That's the least the Brits can do!" Romek raised his fist. "It's about time someone came to our aid."

"We need to hold out a bit longer. I'm sure help is on its way." Peter tried to calm tempers all round. There was nothing they could do about Stalin's or Churchill's unwillingness to pitch in on what might prove a crucial battle to end Hitler's reign. For the moment it looked like they were on their own, but they wouldn't be Poles if they shied away from a hopeless fight. They would persevere.

"Antek is right," Mituk said, referring to Peter by his nom de guerre. "There are two things we need to do right now: hold onto the ground we have gained, and secure the bridgeheads and the airport for us." He continued to explain troop tactics and how he planned to take the strategic infrastructure from the Germans. Unfortunately, the moment of surprise had long passed and to aggravate the situation further, the Soviet air force had abandoned the skies over Warsaw to the Luftwaffe and her feared shrieking Stukas.

"We need better communications," Peter said.

"Yes, I have thought about this and asked Romek to install a network of messengers," Mituk answered.

"Messengers?"

Romek stepped forward. "I have a pool of volunteers from the Grey Ranks, Boy Scouts that know every corner of the capital. They're small enough to squeeze through the barricades and can hope for mercy, should they fall into enemy hands."

"Surely, there must be some other option?" Peter murmured. The Boy Scouts were about the age of his own late son, ten to twelve years old. Were the resistance fighters really desperate enough to resort to children for their communications?

Looking into the grey and tired faces of the commanding officers, the answer seemed to be yes.

CHAPTER 14

August 5, 1944

L otte had been holed up in her office building since the start of the uprising. While the building resembled a fortress and was unlikely to be captured by the insurgents, most of the surrounding areas were in Polish hands and it wasn't safe to go outside.

"It's a nuisance those partisans have to put up so much resistance. As if we didn't have enough on our hands with the approaching Soviets," Lotte's superior, Oberst Braun, muttered beneath his breath.

She heard him and some of the other high-ranking officers discuss the contingency plan, which consisted of waiting for reinforcement troops to arrive, while defending the strategic buildings. After digesting the shock over the early successes of the resistance fighters, they seemed convinced that the Poles would have to surrender as soon as reinforcements arrived.

Himmler himself gave the order to kill every last citizen of Warsaw, not to take prisoners and to level the capital as a warning for the rest of occupied Europe should they want to follow the Polish example.

Lotte gasped as the order came through. She had to warn Ewa. But how? Stuck inside the building and under the constant supervision of Oberführerin Kaiser, who'd taken it as her personal responsibility to ensure the safety of the *Helferinnen* who hadn't been able to evacuate, she didn't have an opportunity to slip away undetected. Frau Kaiser moreover deemed the moral dangers presented by the German soldiers inside the building on a par with the dangers from the Polish resisters outside.

"Oberst, I really wish you could evacuate these girls," Oberführerin Kaiser said for the hundredth time during the last few days.

"Me too." The Oberst looked downright miserable. According to protocol he was required to evacuate all female personnel from battle zones. "But as you see for yourself, we're surrounded by insurgents. Right now, it's impossible."

But apparently the resolute woman had worn down the Oberst with her persistence, because several hours later he gave the order to relocate part of the radio operations and all female workers to another district of Warsaw near the airport that was securely in German hands and much safer than the Old Town, which was the most contested area.

"Sir, will we take the equipment with us?" Lotte asked him.

"No. It's too sensitive to vibration and we need some equipment here. I'll send a delegation to retrieve spare transmitters from the airport to set up in your new location. But I need to find someone who knows to handle it," he said.

"May I volunteer?" Lotte said, hoping this might give her the opportunity to send a message to Ewa.

"You?" He looked her up and down and then muttered, "Oberführerin Kaiser will probably demand my head for this, but since I don't have men to spare and you need to relocate anyway, why not? Wait here."

Minutes later he returned and said, "I have arranged an automobile to take you to the airport and then to your new location in Ohota where you'll meet the other Helferinnen. Pack your things and be outside in five."

"Thank you, Oberst. I'll do everything to your satisfaction," Lotte said and rushed to the basement to grab the few things she owned, before she walked to the back of the building where an olive military vehicle with a fabric roof, called a Kübelwagen, already waited for her. The passenger door opened, and she climbed inside, rendered speechless when she recognized Johann in the driver's seat.

"You?" she asked him, glancing at the backseat where two soldiers with submachine guns sat and grinned at her, introducing themselves as Heinz and Martin.

"Oberst Braun asked us to escort you to the airport for some important radio equipment," Johann said and started the motor. "I don't expect trouble, but just in case: do not, I repeat do not, get out of the vehicle unless I tell you so. Understood?"

"Yes." Lotte nodded.

They'd almost reached the airport when they ran into a roadblock and bullets hit their vehicle. Lotte suppressed a scream and glanced over at Johann. He clenched his jaw, his eyes looking straight ahead.

"Get down," he said without looking at her and put the gear in reverse. But before he could race away, about a dozen insurgents appeared and more shots rang out. The two men in the back rolled down the windows and fired.

Lotte huddled in the foot space of her seat and pressed her hands against her ears. Suddenly volunteering to retrieve the equipment didn't seem like such a good idea. She saw a shadow in the air and heard a loud bang, followed by Johann's voice. "Damn!" He pushed the brakes to the floor and the sudden stop of the vehicle caused Lotte to plop against the passenger seat.

"They threw a metal bedframe out of the window, you can—" Heinz said, but the rest of his sentence was drowned by more shots.

"Can you see where the shots are coming from?" Johann called out to his comrades. Lotte had never experienced him in action, and his grace under fire impressed her. His calm and steady voice helped to tamp down her own fear. With him by her side, she'd survive. At least she hoped she would.

Johann had grabbed his own submachine gun and fired at the men outside the car. Half-deaf, Lotte crouched deeper into her confines, the only sound registering in her brain, the punch of bullets against the Kübelwagen's metal skin.

The stench of Cordite penetrated her nostrils and she gagged. After a few minutes the shooting stopped, and Lotte could feel the sighs of relief of her companions. She poked her head up to get a clear view, but Johann pushed her down again.

"One more enemy at two o'clock, but I can't get a clear shot," came Martin's voice from the back.

"Let's see if we can draw them out. Give me cover," Johann said and opened the door, stepping outside with raised hands. Lotte almost died of terror when she heard him shout, "Don't shoot. I have an injured man over here."

"Step away from the vehicle and keep your hands up," came back the shouted reply in passable German, laced with a heavy Polish accent.

Lotte looked at Johann and she saw the tension on his face. *He's not sure this is going to work, but he's willing to try. Why? Because of me?*

"Where's the fourth person?" their attacker's voice rang out.

"She's applying pressure to the gunshot..."

"Tell her to get out."

Lotte gasped, but when Johann looked at her and nodded, she gathered all her courage to crawl over the driver's seat.

"Nice and slow," Johann murmured without looking at her. She stepped out of the Kübelwagen and stood on the street, her knees shaking, her palms damp, as she watched their attacker step out from behind his cover with the rifle pointed straight in their direction.

"Now?" came the whispered question from the backseat.

"Not yet," Johann whispered back, barely moving his lips. "Wait. Wait."

Lotte trembled so violently she thought she'd collapse to the ground any moment when the insurgent made his way towards them. As soon as he was completely in the clear, Johann sprang into action. He dropped to the ground, pulling Lotte down with him and at the same time he yelled, "Now!"

Heinz and Martin fired at the man standing across the street, who crumpled to the ground into a heap of lifeless flesh. Johann wasted no time. He hauled Lotte up, and shoved her into the Kübelwagen, even as the others jumped out and dragged the metal bedframe aside to clear the street. Johann turned the vehicle and they barely managed to jump inside before he sped off down the street.

"Good job. That was close," Johann said to his men, taking a turn to find another route to the airport.

"We need to radio headquarters about the new road-block when we arrive at the airport," Martin said.

Lotte pressed herself into her seat, her knuckles turning white as she held on for dear life, trying to banish the image of the dead Polish fellow from her mind.

"Are you alright?" Johann asked her as he turned yet another corner to pass through the Wola district. With the main road blocked, he needed to drive through the residential area mostly under German control.

"I'm fine. That was…" she answered with a shaky voice.

"War," Johann said, his hands gripping the steering wheel and a muscle in his jaw giving a tic as he gritted his teeth.

Yet another barricade stopped their journey, but this time it was a German road stop and after presenting the proper documentation, they were allowed to pass.

"Drive slow, they are rounding up every last soul in this area," the SS man controlling the barricade advised them before waving them through.

About two blocks along on Wolska Street, the main road passing through the Wola district, Johann halted the vehicle to let pass hundreds of civilians being frogmarched away. Lotte noticed two SS officers watching the spectacle from the side of the road. One of them was a very long and thin man wearing an ankle-length black leather coat despite the suffocating summer heat.

"Who are these people?" Lotte asked, but Johann gave her only a deadpan stare.

"They're SS," Martin said. "The smaller one is SS-Gruppenführer Heinrich Reinefarth, commander of the Reinefarth Kampftruppe and the other one," Martin pointed, " is SS-Oberführer Oskar Dirlewanger. They've been called in to do away with the partisans."

"Special brigades for the dirty work. Better not to get in their way," Heinz added, and the tone of his voice made Lotte's blood chill in her veins. She swallowed hard, pressing her fingernails into the flesh of her palm, her nerves strung tight.

In front of them black smoke spiraled from buildings set on fire and the sound of intermittent gunfire pierced her ears. Bodies lay everywhere, strewn on the streets like rubbish. SS troopers went from house to house, dragging women, children and the elderly outside, marching them along the street.

"Where are they taking them? What are they doing to them?" Lotte all but screamed, fighting the urge to jump out and do something. Anything.

Nobody answered.

Johann moved the Kübelwagen around the hundreds of civilians, each one looking more desperate than the next, and all clutching onto their most valuable possessions. Women carried their babies. One small child clutched a stuffed teddy bear, its bottom paw torn, the other one well chewed on.

A few blocks down the road they passed an empty lot with heaps of corpses three feet high covering the ground. Lotte gagged as she saw how another group of civilians got shoved inside the yard under the lash of rifle butts. Then she heard the shots of the firing squads that'd been waiting for them.

"Stop!" She screamed, pounding her fists on Johann's biceps. "You have to stop them! Make them stop!"

Johann pushed down the accelerator and the Kübelwagen sprang forward, even as Lotte felt two strong arms grabbing her from behind. She slumped against the seat, whimpering.

CHAPTER 15

Peter spoke on the telephone, trying to negotiate with the Polish government-in-exile in London for some form of support.

"Five days have passed, and nothing has happened. Why on earth is the Red Army stalling on the other side of the Vistula River? Even the constant pounding of their artillery has stopped. What is going on there?"

"We don't know. The Soviets claim their army is stuck on the other side of the river and doesn't have sufficient resources or equipment to make a crossing. They are waiting on reinforcements themselves," his counterpart said.

"And you believe them?" Peter couldn't believe his own ears. Despite assurances to the contrary, nobody gave a shit about Warsaw's fortunes.

The man on the other end sighed. "We don't have any proof to the contrary. Stalin is as committed to defeating Hitler as Churchill and Roosevelt are."

"We urgently need reinforcements and weaponry. Can't you at least parachute weapons into the city?"

Another, longer sigh on the other end of the line. "We have proposed this, but the Soviet High Command won't permit us to use their airfields to refuel nor to fly over territories occupied by them. This severely limits our options."

Peter ran a hand through his cropped hair. In the last few days, all involved parties had spun an intricate web of lies and the Home Army was right in the middle of it. To some extent, he even preferred the Germans. At least they'd always been unequivocal in their intentions: subdue the Slavic race and take Polish soil for themselves.

"We understand your situation, but right now our hands are tied. The best I can offer are airlifts from bases in Southern Italy, but the long distance will limit the capacity of cargo."

"We'll take anything we can get," Peter said with a tired voice and disconnected the call. He'd barely slept in the past five days and his eyelids drooped every time he sat down somewhere.

"And?" Marek asked him.

Peter shook his head. "It looks like Stalin is deliberately stalling. We won't get help from that quarter anytime soon. But the other Allies will airdrop weapons starting tonight."

Colonel Mituk stepped forward, saying, "This is no reason to despair. We've had some fantastic successes and the civilian population has come to our aid. The entire city is united against the Germans."

"Tonight, we'll receive the first airdrops, which should help us arm our troops," Peter said.

"I'll have guards on watch to recover them before our enemy does," Mituk assured him.

Colonel Romek entered the room bursting with enthusiasm. "Our technicians have managed to hijack the public loudspeaker system. Everyone's in for a nice surprise. Go outside and listen." The Nazis had installed a network of loudspeakers on lampposts across Warsaw and pestered the populace for five long years with their propaganda and public service announcements.

Everyone went outside and moments later the national anthem "Jeszcze Polska Nie Zginęła", Poland Is Not Yet Lost blared from the speakers. Peter couldn't help but fight a burst of emotions and when he looked left and right he saw damp eyes all round.

After one hour of much needed sleep, Peter and Marek were ordered to combine their troops and liberate the Gesiowka concentration camp.

"That's impossible. The guards are heavily armed and have a vantage point in their high towers from where they can shoot at us," Marek said.

"You won't say this after you've seen my gift for you," Mituk grinned and took them to the backyard of a former automobile workshop.

"Wow!" Peter gasped as he saw two German Panther tanks standing in the yard and several mechanics cannibalizing one of the tanks to mobilize the other one.

"They were captured two days ago, and the mechanics

swear one's running again and they know how to drive it," Mituk said.

"Knocking on the door with their own tank, I'm sure they'll let us in," Peter chuckled.

"Her name is Magda," one of the mechanics said.

Marek glanced at Peter and rolled his eyes whispering, "Magda? Who gives a Panzer the name of his sweetheart?"

For one moment, Peter felt the old friendship between them return, but Mituk destroyed the moment with his next words, "You need to act fast, before it gets dark. Remember the Germans don't like fighting at night."

Peter gave the mechanics instructions where to go and prayed that they actually could handle that monster and wouldn't accidentally rotate the turret towards their own troops before discharging. About an hour later they joined their battalions, which hoorayed over the excellent booty the Panther represented.

"This is Magda." One of the mechanics grinned as every man in the unit wanted to touch the now Polish tank. Most of them had never seen one except in photographs.

"Let's get to work," Peter said and outlined the plan to his men.

Magda set course for the heavy iron gate of the concentration camp and just like they had planned, the Germans didn't fire at first, assuming it was their relief coming in. That is, until Magda forced her way through two barricades erected in front of the iron gate. Within moments, heavy fire came from all eight guard towers.

The insurgents sought cover behind a building, but Magda was unfazed by the enemy fire and kept her course, crushing the iron gate to the ground and incessantly shelling the towers, until all of them were demolished.

Peter waved at his men to leave their cover and follow the tank inside the camp, capturing the remaining SS guards, firing at those who tried to escape. The skirmish didn't last longer than thirty minutes. Then silence fell over the large compound that had been erected on top of the ruins of the Warsaw Ghetto, which had been razed to the ground a year ago.

In the silence, Peter noticed a skeletal person scurrying from one of the buildings and shouting back inside, "They're Home Army. We're free."

More emaciated figures emerged from the buildings, hesitant at first, garnering courage when they saw nothing to fear. Peter watched one of the most extraordinary spectacle in his life unfolding right in front of him:

At least one hundred prisoners rushed to the gathering place to form up military-style in two long ranks. "Attention. Eyes left," someone called out and everyone followed the order.

The leader of the group approached Peter and saluted, "Sergeant Henryk Lederman," he reported, " and the Jewish Battalion ready for action."

At a complete loss for words, Peter could only nod, while chills of admiration and humbleness travelled down his spine. These brave people had not only withstood the Nazis's attempt to exterminate them, but also they'd refused to be broken and had managed to organize a battalion to fight for their freedom should the opportunity arise.

In the end more than three hundred Jewish prisoners stood in the gathering place and cheered at their liberators.

Most of the freed Jews from all over Europe didn't hesitate for a moment, and joined the ranks of the Home Army to fight the abhorred Nazis.

For a moment, Peter was transported back in time and remembered his first wife Ludmila and his son Janusz. A single tear slipped down his cheek. He'd never see them again. He hadn't been able to save them. The rescue of three hundred others provided nothing more than a band-aid on his wounded soul.

Marek showed up and glanced at Peter, for once not mocking him about taking the easy way out. He put a hand on Peter's shoulder and said, "I'm sorry about your family."

Peter nodded and ordered about half of his men to stay behind and get some rest, while the others would use Magda to secure a communication link between the Wola district and the Old Town.

Later, in their night quarters, a Boy Scout messenger arrived. The young boy brought the newest edition of the Information Bulletin.

"How old are you?" Peter asked him.

"Twelve."

"Take care," Peter said, taking the newspapers and giving the boy a message for headquarters in return.

"Yes, sir." The boy smiled and rushed away.

Peter couldn't help but be reminded of his own son, who'd be of the same age by now. Would he have the same lanky figure as this young boy and the same cheeky smile? Would he also have joined the Grey Ranks and volunteered to become a courier for the fighting units? *Over my dead body.*

That thought sobered him. Deep-rooted grief bubbled

up. He hadn't been there for his family when Janusz had been deported to a death camp two years earlier. From all that Peter knew about the Nazi camps in Poland, children were gassed immediately upon arrival.

His stomach churned, and he hoped his son didn't have to suffer before dying. Despite the nostalgic thoughts, Peter's eyelids drooped, and he gave in to the exhaustion. He fell into an uneasy sleep, haunted by the face of his son. Janusz had inherited the dark brown hair and high cheekbones of his Jewish mother, but Peter's glacial blue eyes.

CHAPTER 16

L otte and her three escorts arrived at the airport and carefully retrieved the radio equipment they needed.

"Aren't we going back?" Lotte asked, when Johann and the other two soldiers headed for the mess.

"Not yet. We need to wait for the commander. I want to personally inform him about the partisans' roadblock." Johann spat out the word partisan like a foul grape.

Heinz and Martin trotted off to greet some soldiers they knew, leaving Johann and Lotte on their own. She picked at her food, the events she'd witnessed still having her stomach tied up and unable to process food.

He noticed and asked, "Aren't you hungry?"

She shrugged and put the fork away, looking into his warm brown eyes, full of concern for her. It was very different from the cold and steely look she'd seen in them earlier today. "How can they do this?"

"Do what?" He looked confused, but then made the

connection to the massacre they'd witnessed. "You mean…? They are under orders to make an example of the people..."

In hopes the resistance forces will capitulate. Lotte silently finished his sentence, knowing full well how the leaders of the Third Reich loved to use terror tactics to control and subdue their opponents. "You could have told them to stop! These people aren't soldiers. They're wives, mothers and children."

"I couldn't have prevented any of this from happening," Johann said, keeping any emotion out of his voice. Suddenly his eyes turned cold and lifeless again, and she hated him for it. *How can he be so indifferent? I thought he was better than the rest.*

"You have rank over these marauding troopers, and yet you refused to rein them in! What kind of man are you? You're as much a monster as they are!" She jumped up, pummeling her fists into his chest, her voice screaming louder with every word.

"Please, calm down," he begged her, but it was too late. They'd already caught the attention of the military police, who came rushing to their table.

"Is there a problem, Fräulein?" one of the policemen said and she stared with disbelief into the muzzle of a gun. Being held at gunpoint seemed to become an annoying habit lately.

"I'll tell you my problem with…" Lotte stopped herself just in time before she told the MP exactly what she thought about the massacre, the Nazis and the Führer. She'd vowed to herself never to act rashly again. Judging by the look on his face she was already deep in trouble. She began to sob. "We…we…were attacked by the partisans earlier and they…

oh God…nobody told me I would be held at gunpoint when I became a Wehrmachthelferin…"

A guilty expression crossed the MP's face and he pointed his gun to the ground, nodding to his colleague to do the same. "Is this true?" he asked Johann.

"Yes, Leutnant," Johann answered. "We barely escaped and had to divert through the Wola district." The MP's brow shot up when he heard the name of the district. Johann continued, "Fräulein Wagner witnessed some of the shooting and I believe she didn't take it well."

"That's why women shouldn't interfere with men's work. They should stay home and raise children," the MP said.

Lotte itched to kick him in the shin, but instead she used the moment to theatrically raise a hand to her forehead and slump against the MP. He had no choice but to drop his gun and catch her in his arms. When she saw his face over hers, she rolled her eyes and then gave him a faint smile. "Thank you. Could I have some water please?"

He helped her sit at the table and ordered the other policeman to bring her a glass of water. Once this was done, he quickly disappeared from the scene, leaving her alone with Johann again.

Johann gave her a once-over and then murmured, "I don't believe for one second you really fainted, but thanks. The military police don't take quarrels lightly."

"I shouldn't have screamed and punched at you. I'm sorry," she said.

"Nothing happened." The warm expression in his eyes returned, confusing Lotte how he could change so much from one moment to the next. She wanted to see the good, caring man in him, and not the battle-hardened soldier he also was.

"Why didn't you do anything? Why didn't you stop the senseless murdering? Do you condone these atrocities?" she murmured.

His eyebrows shot up, but he kept his voice down. "There was nothing I could have done. Unfortunately. Those soldiers you saw, they belong to the Dirlewanger brigade. They're horrible cutthroat criminals and sadists, who enjoy what real humans despise. When their commanding officers tells them to rape, torture and murder, they do it with joy."

"But how...?" Lotte asked, slightly mollified.

"Look, the SS does what they want and Dirlewanger is under the personal protection of Reichsführer Himmler, so he basically has a free hand to do as he pleases. I don't like it, but there's nothing I can do about it." Johann leaned back in his chair, a pained expression crossing his face, before he continued, "I remember one incident that happened in Lodz. We were on patrol, when the SS started retaliation, similar to today. A good friend, Soldat Klausen, gave a wounded Pole something to drink, when Dirlewanger appeared and ordered him to shoot the injured man."

Soldat Klausen. Lotte's eyes became wide, not only because of the atrocious command given, but also because of the familiar name. Could it be a coincidence? "What did your friend do?" she whispered, her hands grabbing the edge of the table with all her might.

"He refused. But one of the Dirlewanger men shot the Pole himself..." Johann broke off, caught up in his memories.

"This soldier...Klausen? Why didn't he shoot?"

"Richard. Because he hated the atrocities he saw, just like you. He could never come to terms with violence against civilians and more than once the others called him a coward," Johann explained.

Lotte's heart raced. Richard Klausen. Rank, Soldat. In Lodz. It *was* him. Her beloved brother. She wanted to jump up and kiss Johann for bringing her news about Richard, but she took a calming breath and plastered a carefully measured smile on her face. Nobody could find out her real identity, not even Johann.

"I realize now that he was in fact more courageous than the rest of us put together," Johann continued. "I wish I had the same determination to stay true to myself, but I fear I've been in this war for much too long. I've become bitter and jaded by what my eyes have witnessed."

Pride rose in her breast at the compliment to her brother, although it was hard to believe they were talking about the same person. Richard had always been an introvert. A bookworm. Not a hero and most definitely not someone she would have called courageous. In fact, as kids, she had been the one to get them both in trouble. She always followed her impulses, no matter how dumb, risky or dangerous, while he remained the voice of reason warning her about the consequences. Not that he'd had much success keeping her from causing trouble all round.

Coward. She'd called Richard a coward more times than she cared to remember, all those times when he'd refused to engage in some outrageously stupid activity with her. Now she felt nothing but pride in knowing that her brother was willing to stand up for what was right. *I love you, Richard. Stay safe*, she said in her mind.

She smiled at Johann. He probably was as torn as she was herself about everything that was happening. Just because he didn't actively get involved, didn't mean he condoned the atrocities. She'd experienced first hand what happened to people who wanted to help those ostracized by the regime. Arrested. Sent to a concentration camp to never criticize Hitler again. She raised her voice to address Johann, "You're a good man. We all have to do things we're not very proud of."

His miserable grin indicated he thought otherwise and she quickly asked the question that burnt on her tongue. "What happened to your friend?"

He gave a snort. "Richard was lucky to get away with his life. Dirlewanger had a reputation for hanging friend or foe for smaller offenses than this. Every Thursday without fail he'd put someone to the rope and take joy in personally kicking the stool from under those doomed to die."

Lotte gagged, and her hand flew to her mouth. She'd thought she'd seen the abyss of human cruelty in Ravensbrück.

"Richard asked his superior to be transferred to a fighting unit. He was a courageous man."

"Was?" Lotte couldn't suppress the tremor in her voice.

"I guess he's still alive. We thought he died in a partisan attack, but then I saw him again in one of the camps...I should have turned him in, but I couldn't. What he did... Why so interested?" Johann shook his head and glanced at Lotte, who had difficulty keeping a straight face, when all she wanted was to squeeze every tidbit of information about her brother from Johann's lips.

"Because he's your friend. I hope he's safe," Lotte hedged. Ever since coming to Warsaw, she'd felt such a strong connection to her brother. *Richard is alive. I just know it.*

"I hope so, too." Johann tilted his head, squinting his eyes at her. "You and him, you'd get along very well. Now that I think of it, you remind me of him an awful lot. You sure you aren't related?" He chuckled at his own observations.

Lotte gave a high-pitched giggle of evasion and quickly changed the subject. "Do you think our drive back will be safe? To tell the truth, I'm a bit afraid."

"Don't be afraid. I won't let anything happen to you." He pressed his hand on hers for a short moment, before another soldier approached to let him know that the commander was now ready to talk to him.

Johann left, leaving Lotte to her thoughts. Would Johann still have the same opinion if he knew her true identity? Or would he feed her to the brutal SS special forces?

She'd rather not find out.

CHAPTER 17

L otte leaned back against the passenger seat of the Kübelwagen, hoping the trip to her new location would be uneventful. She closed her eyes to keep the images of destruction away from her and listened in on the banter of the three soldiers escorting her.

Johann's conversation with the airport commander had taken longer than expected and it was already late. Oberführerin Kaiser had telephoned the airport to ask about Lotte's whereabouts and let them know that she and the other Blitzmädel had safely arrived in the new location.

The Kübelwagen slowed around a corner and ran straight into a barricade. Even before Johann could bring the vehicle to a halt, the soldiers at the barricade opened fire. While Lotte sank to the foot space, crying out when a searing pain tore through her arm. A warm and sticky liquid flowed over her fingers as she reached for the injury.

I've been shot.

As soon as the thought had crossed her mind, loud

voices yelled something, and she glanced up to see at least a dozen armed men, pointing the muzzles of their guns at the heads of the passengers. *Again.* She had to stop being in front of a muzzle.

Lotte blinked. These men were all clad in German leopard-spotted camouflage smocks. Why on earth would they shoot at a German automobile? A rough voice yelled something in Polish that obviously meant she should get out of the vehicle. She blinked again and noticed the red and white armband. Partisans.

Her hand trembled as she raised her hands. Her escorts were yanked from the Kübelwagen and forced to the ground on their bellies. She swallowed hard and awaited the same manhandling when the passenger door slammed open and she stared into the face of a young man with deep green eyes. He couldn't be older than sixteen.

The insurgent seemed to be as surprised as she was and assisted her from the vehicle in a fairly gentler manner, yelling, "A woman!"

A tumult ensued, and she feared for the worst. What if the insurgents had decided to pay back in kind? After everything she'd seen and heard about the rampaging SS troops, she couldn't even hold it against them.

From the corner of her eye she saw Johann and the other two soldiers frogmarched away with their hands held on their heads. Her heart sank at the depressing sight and she hoped they wouldn't face the same fate captured insurgents did.

"What are you doing here?" an older man asked her with a gruff voice in rather good German.

Since she wore her uniform, she couldn't deny her occupation. Neither did it make sense to tell him she was a British spy. They probably wouldn't believe her anyway. "I'm a radio operator."

"Yes, yes, I can see that. But women aren't supposed to be in the battle zones," he said, his perusal of her person stopping on her arm, which now throbbed like hell.

"I…those soldiers you captured, they were about to relocate me to a safer place outside the Old Town," Lotte said. She wanted to put pressure on her gunshot but didn't dare to move for fear of being shot at again.

"Lemme see this," the man said and took a step towards her. When he took off her jacket and grabbed her arm, she winced with pain. He rolled up the sleeve of her blouse and took a closer look. "Bullet shot right through. A bit of stitching up and you'll be fine." He produced a red and white armband from his pocket and tied it around the wound. "That'll stop the bleeding."

"*Dziękuję!*" Lotte thanked him using one of the few Polish words she'd learned, even as she eyed the armband suspiciously. *Does that make me a partisan? Will the next ones to shoot at me be my own people?*

"Take her to the hospital," he ordered the young soldier who'd taken her from the automobile, and put her jacket around her shoulders before he motioned his other men to follow him. Johann and the others were long out of sight, but at least she hadn't heard any gunshots ring out.

The young boy, who looked sorely out of place in his too-big German uniform, made a gesture for her to follow him and said something in Polish she didn't understand. Whatever it was, she'd better follow his orders. Not that she had much choice in the matter.

They walked for what seemed an eternity, her arm pounding with every step she took, until he finally stopped in front of a run-down damaged building and opened the heavy door to push her inside. The amount of suffering she witnessed there appalled her and she instinctively took a step back and crushed herself against the young man standing behind her.

Lotte wasn't faint of heart, but the multitude of injured people, groaning and whimpering, was more than she could stomach after a day like this one. Bile burnt up her throat, making her swallow hard, as she focused on the clear blue eyes of a young girl who'd appeared out of nowhere. Although she was dressed like a nurse, she couldn't be older than maybe nine or ten years. Her short blonde hair was tied neatly with a huge pink bow, and her smile defied the dire circumstances in the makeshift hospital.

"Come with me," the girl said in passable German, weaving her way through the room. Only about a third of the patients lay in beds, with the rest crouched on the floor.

"Take off your jacket," the girl-nurse said, and Lotte did as she was told. She winced at the pain caused by the sudden movement and showed her exposed arm. The girl said with an apologetic smile, "It will hurt." Then she rubbed disinfectant over the wound and all Lotte could do was to press her lips together, trying not to cry out at the stinging pain searing through her arm.

"Thank you," Lotte murmured when the pain subsided, and she noticed the girl had already applied a bandage to the wound. "What's your name?"

"Pauline," she said almost inaudibly, casting her eyes downward. "You can rest over there…"

"Thank you for helping me." Lotte spotted an empty space on the far side of the room and walked over there. Exhausted to the bone, she slumped down against the wall. The wounded men next to her gave suspicious glances at her uniform but didn't say a word. Lotte was thankful for their silence. She'd had enough excitement for one day.

Within moments, her eyelids closed and she fell into a troubled sleep.

The next morning, searing pain woke Lotte when someone bumped against her injured arm. She opened her eyes and saw that a flurry of activities was ensuing as new patients were taken inside. One patient in particular caught her interest. He had short dark hair and wasn't much bigger than Pauline, the nurse. From what she could see, he'd received a flesh wound to his shoulder, probably a grazing shot.

Pauline expertly cleaned and bandaged his wound and then sent him to settle at the far end of the room. When he turned around, Lotte held her breath. The man was but a boy and couldn't be older than ten or eleven. He had a pained expression on his face as he strode over. He wore civilian clothes but had the telltale armband of a Home Army fighter and a huge shoulder bag slung across his shoulder. Soon enough the other patients noticed him and began calling for him.

Lotte couldn't understand the words, but by the proud grin spreading on his face, it was a compliment. The boy opened his bag and retrieved something that looked like a newspaper. When he came nearer, she could read the words *Biuletyn Informacyjny*. Those insurgents had nerve. Amidst a bloody uprising they started printing and distributing a forbidden newspaper?

She couldn't dwell for long on the audacity, because the boy looked at her and Lotte was struck by what she saw – glacial blue eyes that seemed awfully familiar.

"*Deutsch?*" he asked her as he settled in the empty space at her side, and when she nodded, he cocked his head and said in perfect German, "Why are you here?"

"Our vehicle got ambushed and I was shot in the arm," she answered truthfully. "And you?"

"Oh, it's nothing. I've been delivering messages between outposts, when one of the bloody Germans saw me. I dove for cover, but his bullet grazed my shoulder."

She thought it prudent not to remind him that he was talking to one of the bloody Germans and said, "You're very brave. What is your name?"

"Mors."

"I'm Alexandra. You seem so young to be fighting," she commented softly.

"Twelve this past year. They won't let us fight, but the messages we transport are equally important," he said with an air of pride.

"I'm sure they are," Lotte agreed.

Mors was soon up and interacting with the lightly injured, amongst them many children and adolescents. None of them, not even the severely injured, seemed to have lost their zest for life in the face of the brutal battle that had invaded their existence.

Guilt and shame snaked up her spine. They were children, not soldiers. They shouldn't be here. Shouldn't be shouldering the burden of nurses and messengers. Lotte herself wasn't much older in birth years, but in life experience, she felt ancient.

Throughout the day, Mors returned to her several times to chat. He was a fine boy and she enjoyed his company, making her forget that she was a prisoner.

"What do your parents think about you being a courier?" she asked.

"My mother is…she died. And I haven't seen my father in years. Nobody knows where he is." As he spoke, his eyes clouded over. "My aunt doesn't like it much, but I told her it's my duty to fight for my country."

"I'm so sorry," Lotte said, her heart aching for him.

"Where is your family?" Mors asked.

Lotte smiled and threw caution to the wind. "My mother is in Berlin. I have two sisters. They are both married, and one just had a baby."

"And do you have a brother, too?"

"I do. But I don't know where he is. What about you? Do you have sisters and brothers?"

More wrinkled his nose. "No. I wish I did, but first I have to find my papa."

CHAPTER 18

Mid-August 1944

Tom Westlake, British RAF pilot, saw the flaming city of Warsaw appear in front of him. He sucked in a breath, despite the briefing that had told him what to expect. Row upon row of buildings stood in flames, shooting smoke high up into the sky. The dark clouds of smoke glowed in ghostly orange and yellow tones as they were illuminated from below. It wouldn't be difficult to find the designated drop locations, with the night sky glowing as bright as day.

"What a shame," he murmured to himself, and scanned the sky for enemy aircraft. Despite her battered condition the Luftwaffe still posed a serious threat, and he had no intention of reliving his worst nightmare.

"Get ready for the drop," he instructed his bombardier and took his Lancaster down to five hundred feet. Then he saw it. A dark field amidst the blazing fires, marked with torches in the form of a "T". *That must be the cemetery.* It struck him as ironic to drop the weapons onto people who were already dead. But there was neither time nor room for piety in this war.

He'd volunteered to fly the delicate missions from airfields in Italy to provide the Home Army with weapons and ammunition to continue their uprising. It was a nice change to drop things the recipients actually cared for and not just the deadly bombs he usually delivered. Tom shuddered. Ever since his involuntary stay in Berlin, he'd hated this part of his job. It was a necessary evil to win the war, but at what cost?

Tom looked out the window and spoke into his headset "Now!" Flying a slow turn, he saw the telltale glow of twelve parachutes as they carried the canisters crammed with light machine guns, ammunition, grenades, radio equipment, food and medical supplies earthward.

"I sure hope the Poles capture that gear and not the Germans. I mean, it would be crummy to be killed with one of our own weapons," Tom murmured.

"And just how would we be getting shot? They'd need anti-aircraft guns to get us," the bombardier said.

"Accidents happen." Tom shrugged, taking the aircraft up to their travel altitude and turning southward to Italy. Gunfire flashed on the ground and a shiver ran down his spine. Things would be so much easier if Uncle Joe, as the Allies called Stalin, had allowed them to land and refuel their aircraft on one of the nearby Russian airfields. But no, that awful man was stubborn as a mule. He not only forced them to fly the airdrops from Allied bases in Italy, drastically reducing the payload they could carry, but he also kept several divisions of the Red Army less than twenty miles from Warsaw without lifting a single finger.

Apparently, Churchill personally had sent a message to Stalin, begging him to help the Polish, or at least allow the English to help them. But Uncle Joe's response had been terse: basically, blaming the Poles for the hopeless situation they'd maneuvered themselves into by not aligning their actions with the Soviet High Command first. He claimed that the Soviet government didn't want to get involved in this "reckless and terrible adventure" for fear of encouraging "adventuristic actions which might later be turned against the Soviet Union."

Tom snorted. He didn't believe that bullshit for one second. Neither did his Polish air force colleagues, adamant in their verdict that Stalin wasn't one whit better than Hitler, he'd just been more cautious in hiding his atrocious deeds. Most every one of Tom's Polish colleagues had one or more family members on an extended trip to Siberia, courtesy of Uncle Joe.

When the aircraft reached travel altitude, Tom leaned back in his seat. Despite the odd Luftwaffe night-fighter from the training center at Cracow scouring the skies, he didn't expect much trouble.

His mind flashed back to a time more than a year ago: he'd been delivering propaganda leaflets over Hamburg when it happened. Anti-aircraft flak had hit him, and he'd had to bail out. What followed had been both his worst nightmare and his most wonderful time.

Ursula. She'd stolen his heart with her personality and kindness. He'd fallen head over heels in love with her and it had killed him to leave her when the time came. A smile spread across his face and a deep sigh escaped his throat.

"Hey, you fine?"

Tom shook his head and forced himself back to the present. "Yeah, I'm fine. Let's hurry home and get some shut-eye before the next sortie tonight."

The young man gave him a funny look. "Man, I know something happened while you were in Berlin. We all do. But you never talk about it…"

"And I'm not going to start now. I was shot down. Captured. Escaped. Returned to Britain and into the cockpit. End of story."

"You can tell yourself that if it makes you feel better, but I just watched you fade away and the look on your face… you seemed happy. Happier than anyone fighting in this infernal war has a right to be."

Tom didn't respond, but the other man's words rolled around in his head. He had been happy with Ursula during the short time they had spent together. Happier than ever before in his life. And he would be again…after the war. He vowed to return and find her. Make her his wife.

CHAPTER 19

Peter looked up into the sky where small white parachutes wafted in the night breeze, slowly taking their precious cargo to the earth.

"Get ready to recover the drops. We don't want them to fall into enemy hands," he ordered his men. Hours later they had hauled dozens of crates to the ammunition storage and opened the booty with excited faces. Peter looked at his men and smiled. They truly were boys. Not only in age, but also in attitude. And judging by the way they behaved, today could have been Christmas Day. They opened the canisters and found everything they'd been wishing for: weapons, ammunition, food and medical supplies.

A friendly quarrel ensued as to who would get one of the Stens and who would have to do with the smaller guns, but finally every man in his unit owned his own weapon. They had steadily supplemented their meager stock with the rifles of captured or killed Germans. And now the gifts from heaven had fallen from the sky.

He and Marek took a few men to leave the food at one of the street canteens to feed the resistance fighters and dropped off the medical supplies in several of the makeshift hospitals.

"We'll have to hurry to the meeting with General Bór," Peter said, taking a closer look at Marek, who seemed to burst with energy.

"Let's go," Marek said, popping a pill into his mouth.

"What's that?"

"Anti-sleeping pills." Marek grinned. "Want one? I found an entire package on one of the Germans earlier today."

"Sure, why not? Thanks." Peter said, realizing the source of Marek's infinite energy. Trying to remember the time when either one of them had slept for more than an hour or two, he downed the awful-tasting pill with a gulp of water. The effect didn't take long to appear and soon he wondered about the necessity for any sleep at all.

Half an hour later they stepped into Bór's headquarters. Almost three weeks had passed since the beginning of the uprising, but after the first successes, neither side was advancing. Some areas changed hands from day to day, but the hard truth was, the battle had come to a stalemate.

It wasn't that the insurgents didn't fight hard enough – if they ever lacked in enthusiasm, the German zero-capture policy towards the *Banditen* urged them on. No capitulating insurgent was given the status of a soldier and made a prisoner of war, but was shot on the spot. A man didn't need more incentive to keep fighting.

In contrast, the Home Army had decided to honor the Geneva Convention. Peter remembered the discussion during one of the first days of the battle.

"Poland ratified the Geneva Convention and I expect everyone to honor it. This means any German surrendering will be taken prisoner," Colonel Mituk said, looking each of the officers in the eye.

"The pigs deserve to be shot after all they've done to us," Marek argued.

Peter could understand Marek's hatred for the Germans, but if they let their emotions get the better of them, they would never win this war. One more reason why women weren't allowed in the army. At least not in leading positions. "If we do this, we're no better than they are."

Marek glared at him, but Mituk nodded. "That is one reason. But here's another one. Bór believes broadcasting our decision over the loudspeakers will give the Germans an incentive to surrender, and lessen our fatalities."

Peter thought that was a brilliant tactic. As he'd seen with his own men, a soldier who faced execution fought to his last drop of blood and never gave up. Even Marek growled his acceptance but muttered under his breath that he would only enforce this rule for Wehrmacht soldiers. With anyone wearing the black SS uniform, his men could do as they pleased.

Secretly, Peter shared his opinion. Members of the SS had long forfeited their right to be considered humans.

The sound of the door closing brought Peter back to the present meeting.

"We cannot hold the Old Town. It's the most shelled area, and based on the information I get from the commanding officer in that district they're running low on everything. Weapons, ammunition, food, water, medicine," Colonel Mituk said.

"We could stage a breakthrough and evacuate the area," Peter said, not really believing in his suggestion. Like everyone in the room he knew that notion wasn't anything but a wishful dream.

"Not likely. But if we don't do anything, the next Wola will happen," Colonel Romek said.

"What about the sewers?" Marek suggested.

"The sewers? Are you nuts?"

"Our couriers have been using the sewer system for quite a while now to get from one district to the next," Marek said.

General Bór raised his hand to silence everyone. He rubbed his moustache and spoke: "We're talking about thousands of people, not one or two messengers. It would be a huge undertaking."

After a long silence someone said, "But there really is no other way."

"Bring me a map," Bór ordered and someone produced a map of the underground and put it on the large table in the middle of the room.

"There's a storm sewer. It runs all the way from the Old Town to Zoliborz." Colonel Romek apparently knew his way around the hidden parts of Warsaw. "If we secure the manholes here…here…and here…we can place our soldiers and the civilians into the sewer system. We need to use guides to bring the evacuees from the small side sewers into the storm sewer."

The discussion went on for a while until Bór decided this was really the only way, and it seemed viable. Much better than the alternative of falling into German hands. He gave orders to prepare the evacuation of the Old Town and dismissed his officers.

Peter and Marek returned to their battalions, which had shrunk in size to less than half. They had just reached the barricade to their district when bullets whizzed about their heads. Peter dropped to the ground, seeking the cover of the nearby building. A Panther tank rolled down the street, firing out of all barrels, but none of the insurgents returned the fire. When the tank came into Peter's field of vision, he saw something so abhorrent he thought it was a hallucination caused by the amphetamine he'd taken earlier.

Women and children sat atop the tank, effectively providing a human shield for their enemies. No wonder none of the insurgents dared to return the fire. Peter swore revenge and crawled into a ditch to get a better view. He could at least take out a few of the soldiers marching behind the tank.

Of course, his luck didn't last long; moments later, he felt a searing pain in his upper thigh. He knelt on the other leg and continued firing until he'd emptied his entire magazine, before slinking back into the ditch to examine the wound. The bullet had gone right through his leg. Helpless to do anything, he crouched in the ditch and listened to the sounds of the skirmish.

Several minutes later he heard Marek's voice, "What exactly do you think you were doing, asshole?"

"Killing Germans," Peter said, finding it difficult to focus.

"You're plain stupid. And lucky to be alive."

"Where are they?" Peter murmured.

"Gone. Those bastards broke through the barricade, but

at least our men kept them too busy to come back for you. Let's get you to a hospital." Marek inspected the wound and tied a leather strap around Peter's leg before hauling him up and dragging him away.

"I don't need a hospital...just a bandage..." Peter faintly protested.

"Like hell you do. And I'm the one giving orders right now," Marek said.

Peter couldn't answer, because for the moment he needed every ounce of strength to stay upright. The several hundred yards to one of the makeshift hospitals dragged into miles and Peter was almost unconscious when they reached it.

This last skirmish was only one in a long row of defeats. The Germans received reinforcements and supplies on a near daily basis, while Stalin and his Red Army kept the Polish resistance at arm's-length and wasting away. The airlift by the other Allies was a mere drop in the ocean.

CHAPTER 20

End of August 1944

J ohann sighed as he looked out the window of the holding room he'd been kept in since his capture several weeks earlier. The smoke rose across the skyline of the city. Day and night, flames licked at the sky and the smell of smoke was overwhelmed only by the putrid stench of rotting corpses.

The *Verbrennungskommandos*, the civilians forced to collect and burn the dead, couldn't work fast enough to prevent the decay of human flesh in the blazing August sun. He wrinkled his nose, desperate to receive news about the fighting.

Their guards never mentioned a word about the situation outside, except for the carefully measured delivery of Polish victories. Johann had snapped up a few words of the language during his time in the country, but not enough by far to follow a whispered conversation between two guards.

Johann had asked them many times about Alexandra, but either they didn't know, or they weren't allowed to tell him. Guilt tore at his soul. It was his fault that she got captured. He should have been more careful, taken another route, radioed in to make sure the road was clear…He just hoped they were treating her as well as they were treating him and his comrades.

The *Banditen* seemed to be adamant about fulfilling all the requirements of the Geneva Convention, even despite the knowledge that their enemies didn't extend the same military courtesy to them. A chill trickled down Johann's spine. He'd been a proud Wehrmacht soldier and party member for many years, until his army had lost its honor by succumbing to the brutality of the SS and Hitler himself.

His glance crossed the room, which had filled with more prisoners by the day. And for the first time he noticed that all the uniforms were field-grey. Not a single black one among them. What did the partisans do with SS members?

"We need to break out," a young man murmured, coming to stand at the barred window next to him.

"That would be suicide. We are outnumbered and have no weapons."

"Better that than sitting here with our tails between our legs while these Polish pigs…"

Johann gave him a sharp look. "Watch your words. What's your name?"

"Michael."

"Soldat Michael, how long have you been in Poland?"

The young man stood up a bit straighter. "Three weeks. We were the last train to arrive before the pigs cut communications."

Johann forced himself not to roll his eyes. This child thought he knew all about the war and occupied Poland. He had no idea. "Where did you come from?"

"Denmark."

Denmark? That country had never seen a single skirmish beyond the first few days after the invasion. And the young soldier at Johann's side probably hadn't either.

"I'll give you some advice. I have been in the Wehrmacht since way before the war, serving in many of the occupied countries, but Poland is different. These people are fierce. Not deferent like the Danes, or perfidious like the French. The Poles openly defy us, they have staged the biggest rebellion the Third Reich has seen, and they will fight until the last drop of Polish blood has been shed if they need to."

"And your point is?"

"My point is that we are being treated according to international conventions, which is much more than can be said for many others fighting in this war. I have no doubt that our comrades will take back all that has been lost in the first days of fighting and we will be liberated in due time. Until that happens, I suggest you rest up and don't antagonize those in charge of our very lives. We can only return to fight if we're still alive."

Michael stared at him for a long moment, nodding before wandering off.

Johann watched him go, sadness in his chest for the loss of youth Michael had suffered. So many people had lost so much, and after all of the atrocities he'd witnessed in the occupied territories, he was starting to question his loyalties.

He loved his Fatherland. As a young boy he had

witnessed the devastating defeat of Germany in the previous war. He'd grown up with the unjust Treaty of Versailles crippling the German economy and making the people suffer. He'd burned with the desire to take back what rightfully belonged to the country. To make Germany great again. Joining the *Reichswehr*, the predecessor of the Wehrmacht, as soon as he turned eighteen twelve years ago was only the consequential first step.

Johann was committed to fighting for Germany, but it seemed the longer the war went on, the more it deviated from the original intentions. Despite his scruples, after more than a decade, being a good soldier was engrained within his soul. He could no more turn his back on the war effort than he could cut off his own hand. He had to stick it out to the bitter end. Triumph or defeat, it didn't matter anymore. What mattered was that the war had to end.

Suddenly, a commotion at the end of the street drew his attention and he watched as three Tiger tanks rolled into view. Their turrets turned toward the building and he stared into the menacing muzzle.

"Incoming! Get down! Take cover!" Johann yelled and launched himself to the floor, skidding across the room and bumping against the wall on the other side. He covered his ears as a barrage of exploding shells and gunfire erupted outside the building. Concrete and dust fell all around him, but the building held on. With tingling ears, he waited pressed against the floor until the shelling stopped and heavy footsteps thumped upstairs. Several Wehrmacht soldiers with their rifles at the ready stormed the room.

"*Nicht schießen! Wir sind Deutsche!*" Don't shoot, we're

Germans, he shouted at them and slowly got up with raised hands. "Feldwebel Johann Hauser, Warsaw Garrison."

His opponent glanced around asking, "Everyone German?"

"Yes. We've all been captured and taken prisoner. I'm currently the highest-ranking man in the room."

"You're not hiding any partisans here?"

Johann glared at him and, after checking the insignia on his lapels, addressed him, "Obergefreiter. We don't hide enemies. Now get us out of here. I need to return to the *Oberkommandantur* as soon as possible."

And find out what happened to Alexandra.

The other soldier did as told and ordered his unit to get everyone out of the building. On the way down, Johann saw one of the Polish guards crouching against the wall, trying to hide something.

"Get out. You'll be shot, bastard," one of the soldiers threatened him, but the man wouldn't budge.

Johann stepped nearer and saw a tiny hand peeking out from behind the terrified man. "What are you hiding there?"

"No...no...nothing."

"Take that rifle down. I'm handling this," Johann said to the foot soldier, who stared at him in disbelief and didn't move. "This is an order. Take your rifle down!"

Finally, the soldier obeyed.

"Show me who you're hiding," Johann demanded, and the Polish guard shrank even more, pure horror in his eyes, but he stepped aside and a small girl of maybe twelve years looked at Johann, trembling like aspen leaves.

"What's she doing here?" Indignation flooded Johann's body. A young girl had no business being in a combat zone.

"She's…she's…my daughter. She's been bringing in food for the prisoners," the man stammered. "Please don't kill her. Please…kill me, but don't kill her…please." The man fell to his knees and Johann motioned him to be silent.

"Nobody is being killed here. Understood?" he said with a side-glance at the soldier holding his rifle.

Both the German soldier and the Polish guard nodded.

"Get up." Johann had barely finished speaking when they heard hooting and hollering and the German soldier by his side said, "That's the SS coming."

Johann frantically glanced around, and in his desperation shoved the Pole and his daughter into the basement, locking the door behind them, before he turned to walk outside. The marauding SS troopers from the *Kampftruppe Reinefarth* burst inside the building, swarming out to find any hidden enemies.

"There's nobody in here anymore," Johann said, praying they wouldn't find the man and his daughter.

CHAPTER 21

Lotte's injury had fully healed but for some reason she was still in the hospital. Being there reminded her of her sister Anna, who was a nurse. During Anna's training, Lotte had often offered herself as a practice patient, and she smiled at the fond memories.

Feeling bored by her inactivity, and never one to sit idle, she decided to make herself useful. If eleven-year-old Pauline measured up to the task, then, surely, the sister of a real nurse could do so as well. She was feeding one of the patients, who had both of his arms in slings, when the only doctor came up to her.

"Hey, you, what are you doing?" he asked in almost flawless German.

"Making myself useful," she said, keeping her voice low.

"You're German. A prisoner, not a nurse," the man said. He ran a hand through his pitch-black ruffled hair as he stopped only long enough to berate her.

"Above all, I'm human. And since there are more patients than the nurses can handle, I thought I'd lend them a hand."

The doctor scratched his chin as he considered her words. Lotte already knew he and the three trained nurses were overwhelmed with the severe cases and didn't have the time to feed patients or change bandages.

"There's another thing I wanted to talk to you about."

Lotte's heart turned into a tight knot. "Yes?"

"You're no longer in need of medical care and should leave the hospital." He sighed. "We just don't know what to do with you."

She swallowed hard, her eyes getting bigger.

"Since you're a prisoner of war you should be detained in one of the prison buildings."

Lotte hissed out a breath.

"But I talked to our commanders. You're our only female prisoner and I convinced them it wouldn't be wise to put you into the same room with hundreds of angry, frustrated and bored men."

A shiver ran down her spine. She'd never felt threatened by the Wehrmacht soldiers, but who knew how they would behave penned up in a prison camp? Things happened. "You're setting me free?" she asked with a sliver of hope.

"Not possible," the doctor chuckled. "You may seem harmless, but you could still give your people valuable intelligence. So, I asked General Bór to let you stay in the hospital, despite the fact that we need every space for the wounded."

"Thank you. I promise, I won't be a burden. I'll help as much as I can."

The doctor gave her a long look. "Not everyone will like

this, but I accept your offer. Talk to one of the auxiliary nurses about your duties." With those parting words he dashed off to the next one of the severely injured being carried inside and left her alone.

The days passed. Many of the newcomers stared in horror at Lotte's uniform beneath the white apron she'd been given to wear. Luckily, the resident patients had developed a liking for her. In the hospital ward she wasn't the enemy any longer, but just another auxiliary nurse.

Much to her surprise many of the Poles spoke decent German. Once they'd warmed up to her and with the help of those who spoke her language, she could communicate with those who didn't.

Young Mors had returned to his work as a messenger, but he found a reason to come and visit her a few times each week after distributing the Information Bulletin. Each time, he brought a more harrowing story about the atrocities committed by her own folks.

And as much as she despised what her countrymen did, deep in her heart Lotte worried about Johann's safety. He was a Nazi all right, but she still cared deeply for him. Her emotions for him were confusing at best and gave her headaches at night.

Every day more wounded were brought into the hospital, gunshots and burns being the most frequent injuries. Lotte was changing the bandages of one patient when the door opened, and two dirty, blood-covered men staggered inside, one of them dragging the other one, who seemed more dead than alive. She rushed to meet them but halted at the hateful stare in one of the men's eyes.

She backed away as the man yelled something in Polish.

She only caught the words "German floozie" and "You're dead." But that, combined with the menacing tone, was enough to make her back away and slink out of sight. One of the other nurses rushed to meet them and with the help of the mean one she laid the other one on a bed, yelling for the doctor.

"Don't take it personally," Pauline said and put her tiny hand into Lotte's.

"I don't," Lotte lied. How could she keep calm when this man cursed her because she was German? It hurt. A lot. Especially because she'd come to Warsaw to betray her own country and help the Allies. But even now in captivity she couldn't come clean. Her contact person from the SOE had impressed upon her not to let a single soul apart from Ewa know. The fewer people that knew, the safer for her and everyone else involved.

Lotte sighed with relief when the man who'd threatened her left the hospital after receiving a few patches. He'd been filled with so much hatred that it made her shiver. The doctor cursed as he cut off the trousers of the other man and began stitching up his leg. Groans of pain filled the ward. The hospital had run out of anesthetics days ago.

She continued her rounds of helping patients, until the head nurse called, "Alexandra, can you help me please?"

"Yes, one moment." She put down the bandages she was rolling up and hurried to the other side of the room.

"Can you hold him, while I clean the wounds on his arm?"

Lotte stepped up to the bed to keep the half-conscious man still so the nurse could do her work. When he winced, she put a hand to his face. Pained, glacial blue eyes stared back at her, and an expression of shock formed in them when they recognized each other.

CHAPTER 22

Peter thought he'd seen a hallucination. Was the amphetamine pill messing with his head? He gritted his teeth against the pain and blinked, but she still hovered over him. Lotte. Anna's sister.

He muttered a curse, closed his eyes and prayed all of this was but a bad dream caused by the shock and the loss of blood. But when he woke the next day she was still there, hurrying to his bed as soon as he stirred.

"You…Lo…Alexandra?"

"Yes, it's me. I'm going to help you up. You must drink," she said and caught him beneath his arms to help him sit.

Searing pain throbbed through his entire body the moment he moved his injured leg. He clenched his jaw and waited to speak until the ache subsided. "My name is Antek," he said.

"Antek. You have a bad gunshot wound in your leg. The doctor said you are lucky the bullet didn't hit the femoral artery. Here, drink." She put a glass of water to his lips and he downed it in one gulp.

"What are you doing here? Why haven't you been evacuated?" he whispered. He'd been sure the Wehrmacht had withdrawn all the female employees from Warsaw by now. Anna would be so worried if she knew that her sister was in the middle of this awful revolt.

"I got captured by your people," she said.

Peter gave a guilty smile. It should be his task to protect the women in his family, not the other way round. "Sorry for that. I'll see that you're released and returned to Germany."

"First you have to heal," she said, handing him a second glass of water, and lowered her voice. "What are *you* doing here? Why aren't you in Berlin?"

"I had to come here to fight for my country."

"Why do men always want to fight?" Lotte asked.

"I couldn't stay comfortably behind in Berlin while my countrymen are staging the biggest revolt since Hitler's rise. I had to do my bit," he said almost apologetic, hoping she would understand. Wasn't she doing the same thing? Coming here to spy for the SOE, when she could have stayed in hiding at the convent?

"It's not like your life in Berlin was comfortable, you risked your life every day with your *work*. Where is Anna?" Lotte murmured and helped him to lie back again.

"In Berlin. And before you ask, she didn't like the idea of my coming here very much, but in the end, she approved." He tried a grin, but failed miserably, because another wave of pain hit his body.

"How long have you been here?"

"End of July. The uprising was supposed to last a matter of days, not weeks. We were counting on the Red Army relieving us as soon as we had gained the first victories. But no such luck. The bastards are stalling on the other side of the Vistula River."

"Shush," she quieted him, seeing how the anger deteriorated his condition. "What about Ursula's baby?"

He mustered a small smile. "It's a girl. Evelin. I haven't seen her yet, because your sister stayed with your Aunt Lydia. Ursula planned to return to Berlin after the summer."

"Lydia…is everyone on the farm well?"

"They are. As is your mother and her new lodger, Sabine Mahler." He wondered whether he should divulge Sabine's true identity, but decided against it. "Can you give me any information about the German side?"

"We were utterly unprepared. Nobody believed such a revolt could happen," Lotte whispered.

"We had the element of surprise on our side. What other news do you have?"

"Reinforcements have been ordered. Tanks and aircraft are coming."

Peter shook his head, gritting his teeth at the nausea even the tiniest movement caused. "That's old news. The tanks arrived days ago. How long have you been here?"

"Almost three weeks."

"Alexandra, we need your help over here," the head nurse called.

"Go. We'll talk again soon," Peter hissed.

He thoroughly disliked the idea that his sister-in-law was in the middle of the worst street fighting since Stalingrad. But there was nothing he could do. Fatigue returned with a vengeance and his eyelids drooped, making up for weeks lacking proper sleep.

∽

A few days later Marek returned to the hospital to check up on Peter.

"I'm healing well. I guess I can be back with my battalion in a couple of days," Peter said.

Marek stared at him. "That's for the doctor to decide, not you. Where is he anyways?"

"The poor doctor is so overworked he leaves everyone not in a life-threatening condition to the nurses." Peter struggled to sit up. The movement still caused him dizziness. He glanced around the ward to find Lotte and introduce her to Marek, but she had disappeared from sight.

"Is the German slut still here?" Marek asked as if he'd read Peter's thoughts.

"She's a good person. Helping the nurses with everything."

"The only good German is a dead German." Marek stared down at his former friend. "You've been in their country far too long. It's turned you soft."

Peter didn't think he was soft, but it was wiser to keep his mouth shut. He couldn't argue with Marek's unconditional hatred for everything German. "You know, I thought maybe we could let her go…"

"Let her go? What kind of foolish idea is that? She's a prisoner of war! Unfortunately, Bór has decided not to kill the bastards like they do our fighters, but at the very least she deserves to rot in a dungeon for years to come." Marek's voice escalated with every word, attracting the bewildered glances of the other patients.

A nurse hurried over, saying, "Please keep your voice down. This is a hospital." Marek gave a rueful nod, but defiance flickered in his eyes.

"We could turn her and gain valuable information," Peter started another feeble attempt to convince his comrade.

"And why would she do that? She's one of those pigs."

"She's been helping regardless of nationality…"

"To save her own skin." Marek sneered. "The gunshot addled your brains."

"My brains are fine." Peter moved his legs over the edge of the bed, trying to stand up. He failed miserably, and Marek had to grab him beneath his arms to keep him from tumbling.

"As fine as your leg? I'll tell Bór that you won't return to duty for some time. And you stop talking this nonsense about setting a German pig free."

"She's a woman. She doesn't belong in the middle of a battle zone." Peter groaned as Marek settled him on the bed.

"I agree. She shouldn't have come here in the first place. Woman or not, she stays a prisoner until this battle is over."

Peter wished he could tell Marek the truth, but the man would have a fit if he knew that Peter had married a German woman.

"Do you still believe we can win?" Peter whispered.

Marek cast his eyes downward. "There are rumors General Berling's Polish First Army is about to relieve us."

CHAPTER 23

September 1944

Lotte spent as much time with Peter as she possibly could. She liked his courage and determination. And she knew she could implicitly trust him. Despite fighting on the opposite side of the war, his presence gave her security and comfort.

When nobody listened, they shared whispered anecdotes of her family in Berlin. Maybe she felt so strongly towards him because he was the one person who would understand her dilemma with Johann. When Anna had fallen in love with Peter, she hadn't known his real identity either.

Day after day, this question burnt on her lips, wanting to bubble out. But she bit her tongue every time. It wouldn't be prudent to ask. It would only force Peter into an impossible situation, since he would have to advise her to stay away from Johann – the enemy.

"We need a plan to get you back to Germany. You're not safe here," he said one day.

"Probably safer than in Berlin with all the air raids going on," she reminded him, dressing his wound with a new bandage. During her first days as auxiliary nurse she'd felt a strange awkwardness seeing men in their underwear, but with time, the sensation faded.

"Once I resume command of my unit, I'll arrange for your release and see that you have safe passage back to Germany myself," he said.

"Stand up," Lotte ordered him, a smug smile crossing her face when he winced with pain. "Apart from the fact that it'll be a while before you resume command of anything, I won't be of any use in Berlin. Get me out and I'll return to my position as radio operator. I'll send you messages with intelligence from there."

"No way. That's too dangerous. Anna would gladly cut off my head should anything happen to you." He took several steps, wheezing like a locomotive.

"We don't have to tell her that you were involved." The mischief twinkled in her eyes. "I am staying. This is my last word."

Peter groaned, "I've heard those words before. In fact, I believe all the Klausen women love using them."

They repeated the same argument several times over the next few days, until Peter finally caved.

"Here's a special radio frequency the Home Army uses for urgent communications. Use it wisely. And be careful. Don't get caught."

"I won't. I learned my lesson," Lotte said, a familiar excitement taking hold of her. She'd return to action and make a meaningful contribution to the war effort. She might even see Johann again. Whether she wanted or not, her thoughts and emotions revolved around him, worrying whether he was safe…was still alive.

Later that afternoon, Mors slipped into the hospital and sought her out.

"Mors. I haven't seen you for days. I was worried…" She welcomed him with a big hug.

"I know. It's been very busy and the Germans…I don't want to talk about them right now." Mors's lower lip quivered, and Lotte pressed him tighter against her body, wrapping her arms around his small shoulders. This poor little boy had grown up way too soon.

He was stirring in her embrace, struggling to free himself and trying to maintain a worldly-wise expression, when she saw Peter shuffling towards them. The young boy turned to look at the approaching man, when he suddenly stiffened in her arms. His mouth opened, and tears formed in his eyes.

Lotte looked between the boy and the man, unsure of what to do or even what had caused this reaction. Peter wore an expression of utter disbelief on his face and his glacial blue eyes filled with dampness. Before Lotte could process what was happening, Mors escaped her embrace and flung himself into Peter's arms, almost toppling him over with the might of his attack.

"Tata! Tata! I knew you weren't dead and would come back for me," Mors cried.

Peter held the boy close to his chest, obviously battling his own emotions, while the patients in the ward clapped their hands and shouted congratulations at the happy scene.

Lotte's tears spilt over her own cheeks as she witnessed the reunion between father and son.

∾

Peter held the son he'd thought dead in his arms, still not quite believing it could be true. His mind flashed back to Janusz's birth, happy times in Warsaw, and the day he'd left him and Ludmila with his family in Lodz, before the invasion. Then to the notice they'd been taken to the Jewish Ghetto.

He released the boy, smoothing his hands over the youngster's face, a face he barely recognized. He hadn't seen his son for five years, but the eyes revealed who he held. He needed confirmation, though, and hoarsely said, "Tell me your name."

Mors wiped his tears and stood up nice and tall. "Mors."

"Your real name."

"Janusz Stanislaw Piotr Zdanek."

The words dispelled any doubt Peter still harbored in his heart. He hugged the boy close again, taking him out of the ward and to the doorway where he pulled his son down to sit beside him on a bench. It was the best the hospital had to offer in terms of privacy. "Jan. My darling Jan. Tell me, what of your mother? Is she…?"

Jan took a deep breath. "Mama is dead. When they took us to the Ghetto, she contracted typhus and…" Tears threatened to overwhelm the little body.

"But you? How?" Peter asked, unable to stop touching his son's face and shoulders.

"Aunt Agnieska took care of me. She even hid me for a

year and a half, after all the children were deported to another camp in Chelmno."

Peter stiffened at his son's words. That's what the British had told him, that Janusz's name had been on the list of deportees to Chelmno. A death camp.

"Chaim Rumkowski, the head of the Council of Elders, said it was for the best. But my *ciocia* didn't believe him. She said she'd never let them separate us. To avoid problems, she put my name on the list, gave payola to one of the guards and instructed me to hide. Papa, I missed you so much. I knew you'd come one day for me." A bright smile replaced Jan's tears.

"I missed you, too. And your mom." Peter paused for a moment. "But how did you get out of the Ghetto?"

"That was red hot." Jan hopped up and down in excitement. "Aunt Katrina's boyfriend staged an escape plan for Auntie and me. Can you believe it? We escaped right under the Nazis' stupid noses."

Peter smiled. His son might only be twelve years old, but he had the life-experience of an adult. Still, the notion of his baby sister Katrina having a boyfriend didn't sit well with him. Katrina would turn eighteen next month. She still seemed way too young to go out with men.

"I'll have to thank this man personally. Where's your Aunt Agnieska?"

"She lives in Zoliborz. We came to Warsaw with Gentile papers, because it wasn't safe anymore in Lodz."

"I'm so glad to have found you."

The head nurse approached them. "Sorry to interrupt, but the doctor needs to give Mors a message," she said and ushered the boy away.

Peter was still basking in blessedness when a very unhappy-looking Lotte approached him. She didn't wait long to vent her anger and hissed, "Does Anna know you are already married and have a son?"

"Of course she knows. I don't keep secrets from her. I love your sister. My first wife Ludmila died more than three years ago and for all I knew Janusz had been deported to a death camp."

"So, now what happens? Are you going to resume your old life and abandon my sister?" Lotte asked him in a harsh whisper.

Peter opened his mouth to respond, but in that very moment, the doors of the hospital were thrown open and German troops marched inside.

CHAPTER 24

J ohann was taken to Warsaw garrison commander Generalleutnant Stahel in his temporary headquarters. After debriefing the General and his staff, Johann received his promotion to Leutnant due to the death of two of his higher-ups.

He suffered mixed emotions over the news. He'd been waiting for this promotion for such a long time and should have received it many years ago. But that unfortunate incident in Shanghai had stalled his career. His name had never been officially cleared from the accusation of murder-rape. A Jewess no less, as if he would ever touch a Jewess, even if she begged him to.

He scoffed. Nowadays, he'd receive a badge of honor for committing a murder-rape, instead of being accused of the horrific crime it effectively was. He really hated what had become of his army, his country.

Johann returned to his quarters to put the new insignia on his uniform. Once he had, his gaze fell on an envelope hidden in the back of his locker. It contained photographs of his family and his ex-fiancée. The one who'd decided not to wait for him until the war ended.

He fingered through the photographs until he came across the one of his former comrade Richard with his sister. It struck him like a thunderbolt. She was several years older now, but there wasn't a shadow of doubt. The fiery redhead was none other than Alexandra. *My Alexandra.*

His fingers trembled as they turned the photograph to read the note on the back.

Dearest Family,

If you receive this, I'm dead. Know that I loved all of you. But I have a special spot in my heart reserved for you, Lotte, my partner in crime, the one person who always pushed me to my limits. Thank you for being you!

Richard

CHAPTER 25

L otte instinctively stepped forward when the hospital doorway filled with German soldiers, as if she could hold up a dozen soldiers intent on raiding the ward. As far as she knew, she was currently the only prisoner in the hospital. The male POWs always got transferred to either a real hospital or a prison as soon as possible.

"God gracious, a Blitzmädel," one of the soldiers said, beckoning to her. "What are you doing here?"

"I was captured on the fifth of August," she stated, not in the mood to give him more details. Having heard all the harrowing stories from Mors, the safety of the patients preoccupied her thoughts.

"That long? Doesn't matter, get out of here, before the SS comes." He pointed his rifle toward the exit and peeked into the ward behind her back, where the mobile patients were slinking to the door into the basement.

"This is a hospital. According to the Geneva Convention…" Lotte mustered all her strength to keep from swaying.

"The SS doesn't give a shit about anything except booze and dolls. Nurses especially. You should really come with me before they mistake you for one in that smock," the soldier said with a shrug.

Lotte tore off her white nurse's apron to expose the uniform she wore beneath. Panic rolled over her in suffocating waves. Her gaze fell on Pauline, the nurse girl. She couldn't leave her to suffer at the hands of rampaging brutes. Neither could she leave without Mors/Janusz, and Peter, and all the other patients that had endeared themselves to her during the past month.

"Hurry up, girl," the soldier said and pointed at the door where his comrades stood, cigarettes hanging from the corner of their mouths. They didn't seem in a hurry to storm the hospital, but rather enjoyed the small break from fighting.

"Just a minute. I'll be right out. I need to gather up my things," she said with her sweetest smile.

He rolled his eyes at her and turned to ask his comrade for fire to light his own fag. "One minute," he called after her.

She had no idea what to do, but she returned to the ward and found Peter approaching her.

"Get out. Save yourself. Right now," he said, giving her a one-armed hug, before pushing her away. The certainty that she'd never see him again crushed her soul.

Out of nowhere the doctor appeared with Jan, who urgently tugged on her arm. "We can get out through the sewers, but we need time."

"I'll buy you time," she said, picking up a small bundle of medical supplies to make her previous excuse look valid. Turning to Peter she added, "Take care of Jan and Pauline."

"Go. Tell Anna I love her," he answered and herded everyone who could walk to the door in the back of the room that led to the basement and from there into the sewers.

Lotte squared her shoulders and returned to the German soldiers waiting for her. It was one of the hardest things she'd ever done, but she was the only chance Peter and the others had at life.

"All done," she waved her bundle at the man who seemed to be the leader and graced him with a smile. "Would you mind terribly if I took a drag?"

He grinned and handed her his cigarette. "Here you go, Fräulein."

She made a show of puffing out smoke, almost choking in the process. Batting her eyelashes at him, she said, "The partisans treated me well, but I'm still so glad you rescued me. You're real-life heroes. All of you."

That compliment served to loosen their tongues and they launched into relaying all kinds of heroic anecdotes they'd experienced during this awful battle. Lotte wondered why none of them seemed to be in a hurry to rush inside and hinder the patients from escaping. There was no way they couldn't notice how the room had emptied, leaving only the bed-bound patients behind.

"Let's go! The SS is here!" the leader of the unit shouted and grabbed Lotte's arm to make sure she stayed by his side. "God help those poor souls," he murmured almost inaudibly.

"Get in." He helped her into a Kübelwagen similar to the one she'd been riding in with Johann when they were captured. Her stomach squeezed at the thought of him. *I hope he's alive and well.*

Lotte lapsed into silence, praying that Peter and Janusz had been successful in getting everyone out of the hospital and into the sewer tunnels that ran beneath the city.

During the drive across the city the vehicle passed devastation worse than anything she'd seen before, including Berlin after the heavy air raids. Row upon row of buildings stood in flames, burning hot and bright, clouds of smoke reaching high into the sky. She hadn't left the hospital in almost one month, and the shock at the utter destruction of the formerly beautiful capital settled deep in the pit of her stomach.

CHAPTER 26

Peter's heart ached with pride at his young son's bravery, but fear for his safety took over. Jan led them into the basement and through a hole in the wall to a manhole that represented the entrance to the sewer system beneath the city.

Two men worked together to push the manhole cover aside, while Peter sidled up to his son saying, "You sure you can do this?"

"Papa, I have been through the sewers more times than I care to remember, and I will find our way to Zoliborz once we have reached the main storm sewer," Jan said with a firm voice.

Peter nodded. They didn't have much choice either way. Jan descended into the manhole first and Peter's heart squeezed tight as his son's head disappeared into the black hole. One by one, the walking wounded followed him into the tunnel. Peter descended last, pushing the manhole cover in place again. There was no need to let the enemy know they'd escaped.

He closed his eyes for a moment, sending a prayer to the heavens for those he'd brought here and those he'd left behind. It broke his heart to do so, but he had no choice. Without a weapon, even with one, it would have been a futile undertaking to try to stop the German soldiers.

Peter reached the bottom of the manhole and the rancid smell of decay attacked his nostrils. The mucky liquid filled his boots, soaking his trousers until he was submerged up to his bottom. Thankfully his wound had already healed, or he'd never survive the fever that would surely follow after exposing raw flesh to this stinking mass.

Total darkness engulfed him, and he wondered how on earth Jan would find his way. The sewer was small, only about four feet high and two feet wide, and a claustrophobic attack sent cold sweat pouring from his forehead as he crouched down to follow the others.

A high-pitched voice shrieked, the echo bellowing through the tunnel. The man in front of him stopped and Peter bumped into his grimy backside.

"Hush! Do you want to let the Germans know where we are? It's only a rat," Pauline scolded the person responsible in a harsh whisper.

Peter had to smile at the vehemence in the little girl's voice. She was about the same age as Jan, and yet so mature. This war had stolen the childhoods of so many. The group stopped again, and word travelled through the line that there was an open manhole up front, guarded by Germans.

The strain, the frigid water and the disgusting smell made him lightheaded and he longed to reach the open manhole for a whiff of fresh air and light. He put his hand on the concrete embankment, feeling something soft and furry, followed by a squeak. Peter dropped his hand with fright but managed to keep his mouth tightly shut. The rat scurried away, its tiny footsteps drumming in Peter's ears. In the next passage his shoulders bumped against the sides of the narrow tunnel and he had to hunch them forward to squeeze through. For a moment he considered turning back. The sewers weren't meant for big men like him to cross through. He cursed and pushed on.

Thankfully the narrow passage opened into some kind of cave, dimly lit by another open manhole. The group crowded together in the cave and Peter vaguely discerned the small figure of Jan, pointing at something.

Jan jumped down out of sight. Peter struggled not to faint with fear.

Word travelled through the group to grab the guide rope and not let go no matter what. When Peter's turn came, he stared into the whirling water of a much bigger channel that had to be the storm overflow sewer. He grabbed the rope and jumped into the black abyss where the others had already disappeared.

At least the rancid muck had been diluted with rainwater. By the time they reached the end of their journey, Peter half dragged one of the men along with him, but everyone had survived the journey.

"Quiet. I'll check if it's safe," Jan said as they reached another open manhole. Moments later his head reappeared with a broad smile. "We made it."

The Home Army fighters guarding the manhole helped the unannounced travel party to climb outside and led them to a water basin where they could wash off the worst of the muck.

"Who's in charge of this party?" one of them asked.

"Me. Captain Antek. Commander of the Zoska Battalion."

The man raised a brow.

"I was in the hospital with a gunshot. All these people are medical staff and patients. We escaped when the Germans captured the hospital." Peter paused for a moment before continuing, "We had to leave the non-walking wounded behind."

"God bless them. After the Wehrmacht leaves, Vlasov's men come and do their ugly bidding," the soldier said with a very pale nose.

The Kaminski Brigade?" Peter asked.

Although the Kaminski Brigade wasn't technically part of the Russian Liberation Army that fought together with the Germans under the defected Red Army General Andrey Vlasov, the Poles didn't distinguish between them. Both units consisted mainly of depraved Cossacks, Turkmens, Ukrainians, and Russians whose hatred of the Poles was notorious.

Peter had followed the others to the water basin, and was pouring water over his face, hands and legs when he caught a glimpse of Pauline. "Do you have a place to go?"

"Not really." She wrinkled her nose.

"I'll take her with me," one of the nurses offered and Peter gave her a delighted smile. "Thank you."

Within minutes everyone dispersed, leaving just Jan and himself.

"Come, Dad," Jan grabbed his hand and started pulling him down a side alley.

"Where are we going?"

"To Aunt Agnieska's place. She'll be waiting for me already. She always gets upset when I'm late."

Peter smiled and followed his son. Without the adrenaline pumping through his veins, he realized how much his leg pained him and he gritted his teeth to keep from groaning as he limped along the street.

Even though Zoliborz was securely in Polish hands, Peter was surprised at how normal life seemed to be behind the lines. The civilians didn't even turn their heads at the sight of two filthy stinking insurgents. A woman came up to offer them some bread and asked about the new editions of the Information Bulletin.

Soon they arrived at an apartment building and climbed up four floors. Jan knocked on the door three times, counted to four, and then knocked two more times. The door opened, and a face Peter had thought he would never see again appeared. A worried frown on her face turned to a look of stunned disbelief when she saw the two of them standing there.

"Jan? Who…Piotr? Is that you?" Peter's sister-in-law grabbed the doorjamb as her face blanched, and she looked like she might faint.

Oblivious to her shock, Jan pushed his way inside, pulling his father after him. "I found him at the hospital, Aunt."

"You're hours late and I've been so worried. But Piotr… we thought you were dead!"

Peter took her arm and led her over to a chair. "Sit down

and I will explain." He gave her a brief version of the past few years before his strength began to fail him.

"Jan, go and heat some water so your father can clean up. I will find you some clean, dry clothing," she said to him before disappearing into the single bedroom in the apartment. A few moments later, she returned with a bathrobe and handed it to him. "I'm sorry. I don't have men's clothing in your size. That'll have to do until I wash and dry your uniform." She showed him the bathroom. "Clean up and change. I will prepare something to eat. You look unwell."

"He was shot in the leg," Jan said.

"Shot? Today?" Agnieska gulped.

"No, weeks ago. It's mostly healed, but I have to confess our trek through the sewers has aggravated it."

"One more reason to wash and change. You too, Jan," she said with a stern voice, seeing that the boy had slinked into the kitchen in his filthy things.

Several hours later, Peter awakened to find his late wife's sister in an armchair opposite to his, staring at him. "I fell asleep."

"You needed the rest." She smiled. Her pretty face reminded him so much of Ludmila, the woman he'd fallen in love with when he was but seventeen. He hadn't allowed himself to grieve for her, but now the emotions came rushing back, threatening to overwhelm him.

"Where is Jan?" he asked.

"Soundly asleep in the other room. I was hoping we could talk."

"I'm listening." Peter nodded and scrubbed a hand over his beard.

"So much has happened since you left us with your family and went to fight the Germans. Where do I start?"

"Jan told me about your escape from the Ghetto. What about my siblings?"

"Jarek is dead," she said, swiftly picking up the teapot as if to hang onto something. Her eyes cast downward, she took her sweet time pouring tea for both of them.

Peter swallowed. The twin brothers Jarek and Stanislaw were four years younger than him, but he'd been very close to them. "And Stan…?"

"Last time I saw him, he was alive and well. He was the one to arrange for our fake papers and the passage to Warsaw. He's with the partisans in Lodz."

Of course Stan would have joined the partisans. His temper was a force to be reckoned with. Jarek had always been the calmer, more rational one of the twins.

"The farm was torched, but Katrina and Richard managed to escape. I believe they're with one of Stan's partisan friends, helping his mother on her farm."

"Who's Richard?"

"The German soldier who helped Jan and me escape from the Ghetto," she said. "He and your sister are in love. And before you get all angry," her look landed on his balled fists, "Jan and I owe him our lives. I have it on good account that the Ghetto was closed down mere days later and every remaining resident deported to one of the camps." She shuddered despite the warm night.

"She's barely seventeen. She's much too young for a boyfriend," he growled.

"Look who's talking! If I remember right, both you and Ludmila were seventeen when you impregnated her."

"Those were different times. And at least Ludmila didn't fall for an enemy. Why on earth does it have to be a German?" Peter dug his fingers deep into his palms, ready to hate the German who'd dared to touch his baby sister.

"Love doesn't care where you were born or what race you belong to," Agnieska said with a smile.

Peter wanted to argue with her but remembered his love for Anna and closed his mouth. Changing the subject, he said, "You can't let Jan go out on those messenger missions anymore. They are becoming too dangerous. The Germans are taking more ground each day."

"If only I could, but like father, like son. I have as little chance of stopping you from returning to fight as I have with Jan." She stood up with a smile. "It's time to celebrate."

She walked into the kitchen and, after digging around in the back of a cupboard she returned, holding up a bottle of wine in triumph. "I've been keeping this for a special occasion. I think this qualifies."

Peter opened the bottle and waited for her to rejoin him with two glasses, before he poured them each a portion. "What are we drinking to?"

Agnieska was silent for a moment, staring at the dark red liquid in the glass. When she met his eyes again, he noticed the indomitable strength and thanked God that Jan was living with her.

"How about to those that have survived, and those that have gone before us?" she suggested.

"And to a successful end of our revolt," Piotr said, raising his glass. The soft liquid touched his tongue, a multitude of highly nuanced scents exploding in his mouth, sending pure pleasure down his throat. His mind returned not only to his brother, but to his beautiful wife, Ludmila. "I hope she didn't suffer."

"She got sick, it didn't take long..." Agnieska broke off and tried again. "She loved you and Jan more than life. I still miss her, and I know Jan does as well."

"I miss her, too, every day...but...there's something you should know," Peter said, doubt creeping into his mind about whether it was wise to tell her. "...I remarried. In Berlin. A German woman named Anna."

Agnieska observed him across the rim of her glass, swirled the wine, inhaled and savored another sip. "It must run in the family."

"What must?"

"Falling for the Germans."

Peter paused with his glass half-raised and nodded. He couldn't feel any guilt over marrying Anna. He loved her. Not in the same way he had Ludmila, but no less and no more.

CHAPTER 27

Lotte arrived at the German premises, but no warm welcome awaited her there. Instead, two Gestapo officers were expecting her arrival. She was taken to the basement and manhandled into an interrogation room.

"Sit down," the man in charge ordered.

"Why am I here? Why am I not allowed to return to my duties?" Lotte used all her courage to keep her voice from trembling.

"I'm the one asking the questions," he said with a sadistic grin on his face. "Where have you been?"

"I was captured by the partisans together with three soldiers on August fifth." She didn't dare look at him, for fear she'd spring into tears.

"But you were found in a hospital. You don't look injured to me." He stood and walked around her, burying his fingers into her hair and yanking it up.

Searing pain made her yelp.

"Answer." The pressure increased.

"They kept me in the hospital because I was their only female prisoner and they didn't want to put me in the prison with the men." Tears shot to her eyes as she ever so slightly moved her head into the direction of his tug.

"Why didn't you escape?" another voice said behind her back.

She couldn't turn her head to get a glimpse of the other man. If the situation weren't so dire, she would have laughed out loud. *How on earth does he expect me to escape on my own, deep in Polish-controlled territory?* "Armed guards controlled the hospital and the street outside. Besides, I had no idea where I was."

The Gestapo officer released her hair and walked to stand by her side. His hot breath grazed her cheek as he bent down to speak into her ear. "Why don't I believe you? Traitor!" His hand connected with her chin and she was slammed against the chair-back.

"I'm not...a traitor...I was a prisoner..." she stammered.

"I'll tell you what you are." The other man stepped forward, cold eyes mustering her. "You are a disgrace to the German race. A spy for the Polish bandits."

Terror pooled deep in the pit of her stomach. *How do they know? And what do they know?* "I'm no such thing. I'm a radio operator, a loyal employee of the Wehrmacht. A fervent supporter of our Führer." She almost choked on the lie.

"We have reason to believe otherwise. You were seen visiting this house," the first man showed her a piece of paper with Ewa's address written on it.

"My piano teacher lives there."

"*Piano* teacher they call it nowadays? Am I supposed to

believe your ruse? We arrested the Polish snake and she confirmed you're a spy on the same day you so conveniently were *captured* by your insurgent friends."

Lotte shook her head. She didn't believe that Ewa had given her up, but she'd heard enough of the notorious Pawiak prison and Gestapo torture methods to be doubtful. "I have no idea what this woman did outside the piano classes. I wouldn't have taken lessons with her if she hadn't come highly recommended. You can ask my superior Oberführerin Kaiser, she approved of the lessons."

"Another incredibly convenient coincidence, right?" the Gestapo man said, stepping closer to her and piercing her with his cold and cruel eyes.

"What…coincidence?"

"Oberführerin Kaiser left Warsaw with the Blitzmädels weeks ago," he said.

"I…didn't know this…we were supposed to relocate to a safer district of Warsaw on the day I was captured." She couldn't hide the trembling in her limbs anymore. For some reason the knowledge that her higher-up and all the other girls had left made her feel lonely. Vulnerable. Not that they could have helped her… "I really was taking piano lessons. I can prove it. I just learned to play my first real piece of music…" Panic snaked up Lotte's spine. She didn't want to end up in the Nazis' hands again. Once was more than enough for a lifetime.

"Save the lies for someone else." The officer stepped to the door and called for a guard. "Get her out of here. Maybe a night in our hospitality will loosen her tongue."

No. Please don't. Please… she wanted to scream, but her

resolve tightened her jaw and kept her from begging for mercy.

Two guards entered the interrogation room, grabbed her arms and hauled her to the end of the hallway, where they tossed her inside a cell and slammed the door shut. Despite the warm sunshine outside, the cold and damp cell intensified the tremble in her body. An opening in the door let dim light inside, just enough to see that there was no furniture in the cell. Not even a bucket to relieve herself.

Ravensbrück had been bad, but this was worse. She shivered and turned around with the certainty of being observed. Her heart thumping in her throat, she strained her eyes to see in the darkness. Nothing. She stepped deeper into the shadowed corner of the cell and hissed in a breath. A filthy, bloodied man in a German uniform, but wearing the red-and-white armband identifying the insurgents, crouched on the floor. For a moment, her heart leapt with joy.

"*Witam!*" she greeted him in Polish. In the hospital she'd learned to carry on a very basic conversation in this language.

The man continued to stare at her, not even blinking, making her doubt whether he'd even heard her. Just when she was about to say something again, he finally raised his voice and spoke in perfect German. "Kriminalassistent Heller said you were a spy. Just like me."

It would be so easy to commiserate, to tell him everything, to team up with him and maybe – just maybe – find a way out of this rotten cell before the Gestapo had a chance to tear her to pieces. But something held her back.

"I'm not a spy. I'm a radio operator."

He tried a half-smile with his bloodied face and said, "Come on, we're in the same boat. You can tell me the truth. I might be able to contact your counterpart and they can get us out of here."

Lotte tilted her head, wondering why he didn't contact his own counterparts if it was such an easy task. Was he really a spy? "I'd love to escape, but I don't know anyone who could help. I'm a simple woman working as a radio operator and I wouldn't even know what a spy does."

"Look, girl. I'm just trying to help the both of us. Tell me the truth and we thwart the Nazi thugs."

Something in his voice made her wary. "I truly appreciate your offer, but I don't know a thing," Lotte said, convinced he wasn't who he claimed to be. She slunk away into the opposite corner, huddling into a ball, her arms around her legs.

Despite her efforts to stay awake, she must have fallen asleep at some point, because she woke with the awful feeling of being watched. She opened her eyes and noticed the other prisoner standing in front of her and staring at her in a way that made her skin crawl.

"What do you want?" she asked, despite having a pretty good idea of his intentions.

"Tell me the truth. You're my only chance to get out of here and I'm not going to let it pass." He squatted down, reaching out a hand and toying with her hair.

"I am telling the truth. I'm not a spy." Lotte slapped his hand away and scrambled to her feet, fear filling every ounce of her body. She moved as far away from him as possible in the confined space of the prison cell, controlling her urge to cry. Back in the camp the women always said,

"Who cries tonight, will die tomorrow." Lotte assumed this was true in a Gestapo prison as well. Although not crying didn't ensure survival either…

The prisoner gave an angry laugh and followed her. "Why are you lying?"

"Back off and leave me alone," Lotte warned him, infusing a courage into her voice she didn't feel. Once again, he'd backed her up into a corner. Her hands shot up in front of her face.

"I don't think so," he said with a lecherous chuckle. "If I'm going to die because of you, you'll at least sweeten my last night." He shoved her back against the wall and began to tear at her uniform. "Tell me the truth and I'll stop."

For a moment the breath stalled in her lungs, the sound of ripping cloth piercing her ears. By now Lotte knew he wasn't a Polish spy, but a mole for the Gestapo. Although his identity didn't matter. She wouldn't let him rape her.

Her time in the convent hadn't been spent exclusively praying and helping with the orphaned children. Actually, most of the time she'd trained for situations just like this one.

She waited until the filthy man had shoved her skirt up to her waist and leaned closer to press his hard body against hers. Only then did she raise her knee, driving it into his groin as hard as she could while shoving him backwards with both hands.

He howled in pain, grabbed his crotch and fell to the ground, gasping for breath and huddling in a fetal position.

"I asked you to leave me alone," Lotte said.

"You'll regret not playing nice with me. There are much

worse things awaiting you than sleeping with me," he howled.

Lotte didn't answer and was attempting to move around him when his hand shot out and gripped her ankle, unhinging her equilibrium. She spat at him, yanking her ankle away and yelling, "I'm innocent! But you…you are a lowlife criminal and deserve to be locked up in here! Your behavior is shameful and an insult to every other man!"

He crawled to the other side of the cell, still holding his crotch, screaming, "You bitch! I'll make sure you regret not being friendlier to me!"

She ignored him, smoothed her skirt back down and retreated into the opposite corner, hissing a final warning. "Touch me again, even come near me, and I'll make sure you never use what you're holding again. I'll kick you so hard that your groin comes out your throat."

This time she forced herself to stay awake. She couldn't let exhaustion overwhelm her and give him the advantage, so he could rape her while she was defenseless in her sleep. In the wee hours of the morning, heavy footfalls indicated the return of her captors.

"Did she talk?" one of the guards asked.

"No," the prisoner answered as he was hauled away.

Despite his devious behavior Lotte felt a tiny pang of empathy for him and what awaited him now at the Gestapo's hands.

They left her to rot in the damp cell without food or drink. Lotte lost track of time, her thirst so unbearable she licked the moisture from the walls. When they came for her again, she had no idea whether mere hours had passed or entire days.

"Did you have some time to think?" the Gestapo officer, who must be Kriminalassistent Heller, asked her, shoving her harshly into the interrogation room.

Lotte set her jaw tight and gave him a dark stare in return.

"Well, well. Looks like you're one stubborn bitch. But make no mistake, I always get what I want. It just takes longer sometimes."

"I'm not a spy. I have never done anything to damage Germany."

"Is that so?" Heller loomed over her with a smug smile.

Lotte didn't see it coming and yelped when he struck her face.

"It's about time you started talking."

"I'm innocent. I swear," Lotte murmured, flicking out her tongue. The metallic taste of blood assailed her senses and dread flipped her stomach over.

"Who are your contact persons? Who are you working for?" Question after question rained down on her, only interrupted by slapping, punching and kicking.

"I'm not a spy…I'm a radio operator for the Wehrmacht," Lotte repeated again and again, until two meaty hands gripped her neck. She choked in panic, ready to tell him everything he wanted to know, if only he'd let her breathe again.

She must have fallen unconscious because she woke from chilled water running down her head and gasped.

"Ready to tell me your contacts?" Heller asked.

"I don't know anything or anyone. I never knew this woman was anything other than a piano teacher."

"You will talk!" the officer shouted at her, his face

becoming beetroot-red, and she feared he'd kill her right there and then. But much to her surprise he turned on his heel and left the room, leaving Lotte alone with her aching body.

Rough rope bound her hands, tied behind her back, and her ankles were chained to the legs of the chair. Licking the blood from her lips, she blinked. Her left eye was swelling rapidly, impairing her vision and removing the ability to keep it open. Hunger pains attacked her stomach, causing unwelcome memories to appear. Through her haze she saw a gaunt and bald woman look at her. *Verena!* This couldn't be real. The woman, who'd taken her under her wing in Ravensbrück and taught her to survive, couldn't be here.

"You must focus. Find your strength inside," Verena said.

Lotte blinked, and the room was empty. She focused on sitting upright, her chin held high. The Nazis could torture her all they wanted. She'd never give her friends away. After an eternal time in agony, the door opened again, and her interrogator returned. Two guards trailing behind dragged a bruised and bloodied man between them.

His head slumped downward. His uniform with the Polish armband was torn apart, exposing cuts, bruises and burns on his entire body. Lotte cringed when they threw him at her feet and he moaned in pain.

"Look at what happens to those who lie to us. Wake him up," Heller commanded.

A guard approached with a bucket of water and emptied it upon the prisoner. "Get up!"

The poor man stumbled to his feet and Lotte's heart froze when she saw his face. Recognition hit his brown eyes the same moment it hit her. *Marek! Peter's comrade. What kind of sick game are they playing here?*

"Look at her. Is she a Polish spy?" the Gestapo officer demanded.

Marek stared at her, one eye swollen shut. He gave her a hateful look and then spat at her feet. "She's a filthy German."

The officer slapped him. "For all we know she's working for the Home Army. She posed as a nurse in the hospital we liberated."

"Liberated? You bastards killed everyone!" Marek hadn't even finished his sentence when the officer's fist connected with his ribs. A pitiful groan echoed through the room.

Lotte instinctively wanted to raise her hand to cover her mouth, but the movement was stopped by the coarse rope cutting into her wrists.

"So, you don't deny knowing this woman?"

Marek righted himself before he answered. "I don't know her. I saw her once at the hospital. Our people should have killed her instead of taking her prisoner."

An evil smile spread across Heller's face and his voice became velvety. "Suit yourself. I'm willing to indulge your revenge. Kill her, and you go free."

Lotte watched Marek's face, seeing the stunned look as the officer's words registered in his brain. She was as good as dead. Even against the tortured and weakened man she didn't stand a change. This Marek wasn't a flimsy wimp like the mole they'd planted in her prison cell.

Heller winked, and another Gestapo brute stepped forward, pressing a knife into Marek's hand. "Kill her, if she's not a spy. Or spare her life if she's one of yours."

CHAPTER 28

Johann was having lunch with the commanding officer of the Warsaw Garrison. He'd been tasked with making strategic plans for the time after this rebellion ended. Johann had had enough time to think during his captivity and he'd come to the conclusion that the insurgents couldn't be defeated with cruelty. Those stubborn people were determined to fight to the last drop of blood.

In his point of view there was only one way to stop the shedding of innocent blood while keeping at least some of the residents alive.

"Sir, we might want to cede the partisans the status as soldiers—"

"Hell no, they're criminals and deserve to be shot on the spot," the Kommandant said.

"I know, and I fully agree with your opinion, but...may I present an idea, please?" Johann tried again.

"Speak." His superior took another forkful of minced meat.

"For whatever misleading reasons the partisans think they can still win their little revolt. And to tell the truth, they have been more than a mere nuisance for us. Instead of turning our focus to pushing back the Red Army, our men are engaged in house-to-house fighting in this damned city. If we offer the insurgents the military courtesy extended to soldiers of a regular army, and that means taking them prisoner instead of shooting them, they might be inclined to surrender. And..." Johann paused to put his ace on the table, "...our country needs laborers. These men will be of better use to us working in the Reich than dead and buried here."

The Kommandant glanced up from his plate of food, snapping his fingers. Several moments later, a servant appeared. "Yes?"

"Bring me wine!" The commander turned to scrutinize Johann. "That's actually a brilliant idea. It's about time the depraved *Kampftruppe Reinefarth* unleashed their terror against the Red Army instead of harassing civilians."

"Thank you, sir," Johann said, sipping the wine. He wondered how he could broach another topic that weighed on his heart. Since his liberation from captivity, Johann had discreetly inquired about Alexandra Wagner.

Nothing. She was like a ghost, only the bare essentials known about her. A person who'd never appeared in public until the day she turned eighteen about six months ago. Incidentally, that was around the time Richard Klausen's sister, Lmotte, had died.

"Sir, you may remember that when we were captured by the insurgents, there was a Blitzmädel with us. Did you ever find out what happened to her?"

The Kommandant looked at Johann as if he'd seen a

monster. "Why on earth would you inquire about *her*?"

Something was awfully wrong. Johann's stomach churned, and judging by the commander's menacing tone, he was treading on thin ice. "It's just that I feel guilty, because she got captured on my watch. I couldn't protect her."

"You don't have to feel guilty. Our friends from the Gestapo captured a woman named Ewa Gusten who works as a spy for the British. Fräulein Wagner was a mole. She's been seen visiting her frequently."

Johann suppressed a gasp hearing the name of Alexandra's piano teacher and willed his features to remain neutral, as he answered, "Has this Ewa Gusten confirmed names?"

The Kommandant shook his head. "Unfortunately not. Our lads were a bit too enthusiastic with their interrogation and she died before she could spill names. We only have her frequency and call sign."

"I see…" Johann didn't see anything except that Alexandra was in deadly peril.

"…the Blitzmädel is a spy. For the Polish. Or the British. It really doesn't make a difference. The whole capture by the partisans was staged by her just so she could escape punishment. But the Gestapo never loses a guilty offender. She'll get what's coming to her and then some. In fact, you might find pleasure in punching that traitorous bitch in the face."

Johann tuned out every emotion and said, "I'm glad the Gestapo arrested her. And if you think I might be of use to the interrogation, I'm more than willing to do my bit… while taking my personal revenge."

CHAPTER 29

P eter left Agnieska's apartment in Zoliborz early in the morning to report to General Bór's headquarters, which happened to be in the same district, one of the few still in Polish hands. He passed burnt-out ruins and buildings with huge shell holes in them. It amazed him that any of the structures still stood upright.

Six weeks ago, the civilians had been thrilled at the prospect of liberation, working alongside the resistance fighters building barricades. Housewives had ventured into the streets offering freshly baked bread and cool beverages to the fighters.

But today the streets reeked of mournfulness. Corpses lay piled among the rubble, small crosses marking the graves of others. The skirmishes had dragged on for such a long time that people had lost their enthusiasm.

"It's all your fault!" a crying mother accused him as she cradled her dead child in her arms. "Why did you have to go up against the Nazis? Look what you've done!"

Peter sped up his steps. He had no words of consolation for her, nor did he care to defend the decision to rebel. Nothing had worked out according to plan, and perhaps it was time to close this chapter and try to salvage those still alive.

When he entered the basement serving as headquarters, heads snapped around, looking at him like they'd seen a ghost.

"Antek? We thought you'd been killed in the hospital," Colonel Romek said.

Apparently, the soldier guarding the manhole hadn't passed on the information. Lack of proper communication between units had been one of the main problems since the beginning of the uprising. That was one of the few things Peter admired about the Germans; they were always supremely well organized.

"I escaped with the staff and the walking wounded through the sewers," Peter answered.

"Good. Then you can take over your old battalion and Marek's," Colonel Mituk said.

"What's with Marek?" Peter asked, sensing an invisible hand squeezing his chest.

"Captured by the Gestapo."

Peter slumped in a vacant chair. He and Marek hadn't been on the best of terms during these last weeks, but that didn't change the fact that he still cared for his former friend. No one deserved torture and death at the hands of a brutal enemy.

Another officer rushed into the room with news. "The Germans announced they won't shoot those who surrender but take them as prisoners of war."

Peter scoffed. "And that's supposed to be a good thing?"

"It is. General Bór has been negotiating with General von dem Bach on the conditions of a possible capitulation," Mituk said.

"Capitulation?" Peter felt all the blood draining from his face. *How could they?*

"It's just preliminary negotiations, but we're losing men, weapons, everything, including support in the populace. There's been too much bloodshed. Our fatalities are in the hundreds of thousands. To aggravate the situation further, the Luftwaffe is dropping propaganda leaflets, asking everyone to capitulate before the city is destroyed in an unnecessary battle. People are tired, starved and hopeless," Romek said.

Peter nodded, his lips quivering as he tried to control his emotions. He felt betrayed. Not by the civilians, nor by his commanders who sought the best for their country. Not even by the Russians who'd taken the first opportunity to stab a knife into Poland's back. Russia had always been a foe, so this kind of treason had to be expected.

No, he felt betrayed by Poland's so-called allies. The British. The French. The Americans. How had they responded to the Home Army's desperate pleas for help? By dropping a few weapons here and there. Nothing to speak of. With every passing day, the Home Army was pushed further into the corner, while the Germans gained the upper hand. And the way things were going, he feared he'd never see his beloved Anna again.

CHAPTER 30

I n the interrogation room, Lotte warily watched Marek, fully expecting him to shove the knife between her ribs at any moment. She stared at him, willing him to be strong and to make his strike quick and effective.

But the damned man stood in the middle of the room, surrounded by four Gestapo officers with rifles pointing at him. The knife held loosely in his hand, as if he pondered his choices.

"Kill her if she's not a Polish spy," Kriminalassistent Heller demanded.

Marek shook his head. "She's a filthy German, but I won't kill an unarmed woman. I'm not a cowardly monster like you bastards."

Heller raised the leather lash in his hand and struck Marek across the chest.

"Don't hit him, please!" Lotte yelped. But the enraged Gestapo officer raised his lash again and again.

Despite the vicious attack, Marek stood – swaying, yet

upright – holding Lotte's gaze. The determination and resignation of an entire nation expressed itself in his dark eyes. In that moment it struck her that they'd never let him go free, even if he killed her. Both of their fates were sealed. She knew it and Marek knew it, too.

It wasn't a matter of life or death anymore; it was merely a matter of honorable or shameful death. Tears ran down Lotte's face when she realized what he was about to do.

Marek's hand tightened around the knife and before Heller could knock him down with yet another strike of the lash, he lunged at the Gestapo officer in a hopeless attempt to turn the tables. He must have known this action would get him killed, because he didn't look surprised when bullets riddled his body and he dropped mid-air before reaching his target.

Lotte's vision grew dim as she tried in vain to tear her eyes away from the dying man, who'd sacrificed himself for her. The familiar curse of guilt swallowed her, blocking out every other emotion. Another person lay dead at her feet. And she'd done it. Her. She'd never, ever forgive herself for Marek's death.

Lotte woke with a chill. Goosebumps exploded on her skin as icy droplets of water ran down her body. Her hair and clothes were soaked, clinging to her and making her shiver. She opened her swollen eyes and it took her a minute to recognize where she was.

Tied to a chair in the interrogation room – Marek's corpse lying at her feet. Bile rose in her throat and she would surely have vomited if she'd had anything to eat since being thrown into prison God knows how many days ago.

"Good, you're back with us." Kriminalassistent Heller stepped into her view and took her chin into his hand, yanking it up to force her to hold his stare. "That bloody partisan was a fool. I trust you will be wiser. We know that you are a spy. You can save yourself by revealing to us the names of all your contacts in the resistance network."

Her mind raced, violently spinning in every direction. She wouldn't endanger anyone else. She couldn't. Two of her best friends had been killed because of her rash actions...before...before she became Alexandra. This new and improved version of Lotte wouldn't let this happen again.

"I've told you before. I'm not a spy. I have no idea what you're talking about. I've never had any contact with anyone from the resistance."

"Stop lying to me!" Heller yelled in her face, slapping her and splitting her lip in the process.

Her mouth filled with blood and she shook her head. "I don't know what you're talking about. I'm a radio operator. I volunteered because I wanted to help the war effort."

Heller sneered at her, leaning his face so close, she could see the dark speckles of bristles on his freshly shaven face. "You have a decision to make, Fräulein Wagner. Face the firing squad or expose your contacts. Really simple if you ask me. Your life or theirs. Think about it."

"I can't tell you my contacts because there are none," Lotte said, forcing down the sob rising in her throat.

He shook his head and made a *tsk*ing sound. "Firing squad? So be it. Take her back to her cell."

Lotte didn't care that they untied her wrists and ankles, hauled her to her feet and manhandled her back to her cell. She didn't care that they joked all the way and argued about who'd get first dibs at shooting her. And she didn't even care that the male prisoner who had tried to rape her the night before was gone, and she had the cell all to herself.

She huddled in the corner of the cold, damp prison, resigned to making amends for every wrong she'd done in her life, praying to God that Peter, Jan, Pauline and all the others would stay safe. She had no idea how long she'd been sitting in the semi-darkness when a soft voice called her name. Her roommate Gerlinde stood in the cell, holding a glass of water and a chunk of bread in her hands.

I must be hallucinating. She left with all the other Helferinnen weeks ago.

"Alexandra. Look at you," Gerlinde whispered, squatting next to her and handing her the food.

"For me?" Lotte greedily gulped the water and stuffed the entire piece of bread into her mouth, fearing someone could snatch it away from her again. She bit down chunks and stored them in her cheeks for later, savoring the hard bread, chewing, salivating, chewing – swallowing down tiny bits the way she'd learned from Verena in the camp. The bread changed its texture and became soft and mushy, the dough turning sweet as the starch dissolved into sugar.

"How did you get in here and why?" Lotte asked, suspiciously eyeing her friend. Was Gerlinde the one who'd ratted on her? Lotte racked her brain. She'd always been careful, Gerlinde couldn't have known that Ewa was anything but her piano teacher.

"Kriminalassistent Heller sent me to talk some sense

into you. Be reasonable, please. Just tell him who your contacts are, and he'll let you go."

"Is that what he told you? That he's going to let me go?" Lotte laughed ruefully, the sweetness of the chewed bread filling her mouth and making her feel almost giddy.

"Yes. Heller said you'd go free if you tell him what he wants to know."

"I can't tell them what I don't know." Lotte kept up her pretense of innocence. The Gestapo couldn't be trusted. If she told Heller what he wanted to know, he'd turn around and kill her anyway. She'd seen and heard it happen too many times.

"Why are you still here?" Lotte asked, "they told me all other females have been evacuated."

Gerlinde cast her eyes downward and it was only then that Lotte heard the steps of a guard obviously lingering behind the locked door. "I missed the train on purpose. They were going to send me to a great-aunt who's a nun. I wasn't going to a convent for anything in the world. Oberst Braun was livid when he found out, but there was nothing he could do."

Lotte rolled her eyes. This woman didn't seem to have a modicum of common sense in her bones.

"And..." Gerlinde put her hand on Lotte's arm. "I didn't want to leave without you in case you needed me."

"Aww...thanks." Lotte still wasn't sure whether she could trust her friend. Apparently Gerlinde was here with good intentions, but she couldn't be sure. Maybe she'd worked for the Gestapo all along?

"Seems like I was right. Now will you tell the Gestapo what they want to know?" Gerlinde begged with tears in her eyes. "Please. Just expose your contacts and the guard will let you walk out of here with me."

Lotte shook her head. "I can't. I don't know anything."

"Come on. Don't be so stubborn. Just invent something. Don't you know anyone who could be a part of the resistance? Maybe the cleaning lady in our previous office?" Gerlinde suggested.

"And risk having the poor woman killed? I'd rather die than be responsible for the death of innocent people," Lotte said, mimicking what Marek had done for her earlier. He'd despised her so much and still he'd spared her life. Now she would follow his example.

Gerlinde choked back a sob; unshed tears shining in her eyes. "I'm so sorry. I wish you'd told me. Kriminalassistent Heller promised you'd go free if only you gave him names." She called for the guard to let her out, turned back at the last minute and blew Lotte a kiss. "Goodbye, Alexandra. I wish…" She covered her mouth as another sob rose up and she rushed away. The guard slammed the door shut, leaving Lotte alone once again with her turbulent thoughts and emotions.

Shame. Regret. Resignation.

She sat there, listening as her friend's footsteps faded away, knowing in her heart of hearts that she'd made the right choice.

CHAPTER 31

Peter paced the room, a deep frown on his face.

"You sure you didn't catch anything on that frequency?" he asked the radio operator Lis, a beautiful woman in her thirties with raven hair, for the umpteenth time.

"I'm perfectly sure," she said, giving him a saccharine smile that could as well mean she wanted to strangle him. "And if you'd stop pacing, please, I could concentrate on deciphering the Morse code."

"Sorry," he said and left the room.

Several days had passed with no news from Lotte. Nothing. No transmissions. No notice. The worry about her clouded his mind. If anything happened to her, Anna would never forgive him. *Anna.* He smiled at the memory of her delicate skin, her sharp mind and her unwavering determination. Anna and her older sister Ursula might look alike, but it was fledgling Lotte who shared many of Anna's character traits. Determination. Fighting spirit. And a kind heart.

He missed Anna. A lot. And with every passing day the worry plaguing him that he'd never see her again etched itself deeper into his soul. The least he could do was to see her sister safe. If needed, he'd shackle Lotte to a seat on a Berlin-bound train and get her out of the hellhole his beloved Warsaw had become.

Ewa. Hadn't Ewa mentioned a German girl coming to take piano lessons? What if the German girl was Lotte and Ewa her contact person? His breath caught in his lungs. *It's worth a shot. No, it's too dangerous. You might compromise Ewa. But I need to know what happened to Lotte.*

Against his better judgment he put on his smock and walked to Ewa's house. The building lay in one of the most embattled areas of town and more than once he had to dive for cover as mortar fire rained down on him.

"Hey, where are you going?" an insurgent called out to him.

"Visiting a friend," Peter answered, not willing to give away more information than needed.

"There are no friends over there anymore. The Germans regained this street weeks ago. We're holding as best as we can to give people from the City Center a chance to escape."

Peter looked through a peephole in the barricade onto the building where Ewa had lived. It was a ruin, burnt to the ground, its blackened remains reaching up into the sky like a hand begging for help. Nobody lived in that building anymore.

"Do you know what happened to the residents?" he asked his new friend.

"Not much. Most fled the city during the two-hour cease-fire negotiated by the Red Cross. But rumors have it that one woman was an informer for the British. The Gestapo got her. Bastards." The soldier cursed and ducked as bullets flew over their heads.

"Thanks, lad." Peter crawled backwards until he'd reached safe cover behind a building. *So much for finding Ewa.* Worse, if she'd been captured, and talked under torture, Lotte was in serious trouble by now. He decided to return to Agnieska's place. The two of them had some talking to do.

Jan jumped at him, giving him a bear hug, as soon as he opened the door of the apartment. Peter smelled freshly baked bread and his stomach growled in response. Food was getting scarce in the city.

"Hello, big one." He greeted his son and set him down, before taking off his smock. "Where's your aunt?"

"Making dinner. Can you tell her not to make barley again?" Jan made his request with a grimace. Since the resistance had captured a brewery, malted barley was the only thing that could be obtained in decent quantities.

"I'm sorry, but Agnieska has to make do with whatever rations she can get."

Peter stepped into the kitchen, where his sister-in-law was putting some nondescript weeds into a pot with boiling water. He shuddered and chose not to inquire what she was cooking.

After dinner, he tucked Jan into bed with a kiss on his forehead and returned to the living room to find Agnieska waiting for him in one of the armchairs, two mugs of steaming tea on the small table.

"You look like you need to talk," she said quietly.

Peter nodded and sat in the other chair. "I went to see my contact, but the area is now under German control and it seems she was arrested by the Gestapo."

"They'll be looking for anyone who had contact with her," Agnieska warned him.

"I know that." *And it worries me, but not so much for myself.* He paused, taking a sip of his tea. How could he best broach the delicate topic? Head-on, he decided. "Who will take care of Jan if something happens to either one or both of us?"

Agnieska nodded, her brow furrowed. "I've thought about that countless times. The elderly lady next door will take him in for a few days, but then...I haven't been able to contact Katrina or Stan since they had to flee the farm."

"Isn't there anyone else? From your side of the family?" Peter asked.

"My side?" She scoffed at him, endless melancholy entering her eyes.

"I'm sorry." Peter apologized for his carelessness. Agnieska's entire family had been deported to various ghettos and camps long ago for being Jewish.

"We don't have many friends left in Warsaw. Most are either dead or escaped," Agnieska said. "What about your new wife?"

Peter shook his head. While he was sure Anna would welcome his son with open arms, it wasn't a viable option. An orphaned Polish boy would be shot before he ever set foot into Germany.

"Then we just have to stay alive," Agnieska said.

CHAPTER 32

Lotte woke from a fitful sleep when an armed guard entered her cell, delivering water and bread as well as pen and paper. Was she really going to write her last letter? Tears threatened to spill down her face, but she refused to give her captors the gratification of seeing her cry.

"Here, write. I'll be back soon," the guard said.

She gulped down the water and chewed the bread, this time not saving anything for later. The white sheet of paper seemed to mock her, and she swallowed hard as she realized that this stupid paper represented her last chance to express her feelings for her family.

Far from it.

Alexandra Wagner was an orphan and if she broke her cover now, she'd endanger the very persons she loved so much. Tears slipped down her cheeks. A fat lot she cared! She'd die today anyway so she could bawl as much as she wanted.

Dearest Anna,

Thanks for being such a good friend. So many things have happened that I'd love to share with you, but you won't hear from me again.

I'm beyond sad that I have to leave this earth today. When you receive this letter, I'll be long gone, but know that I have lived life to the fullest and don't regret one moment of it.

The one thing I do regret is not having a family that I can hug in this moment of despair. Please don't believe anything you hear about me. The Gestapo is convinced I'm a Polish spy, which I'm clearly not.

Give my love to your family, who's always been so kind to me.

All my love,

Alexandra

PS: I have met a wonderful man here in Warsaw, a dashing soldier with glacial blue eyes. Last I saw him he was well and alive. You'd love him.

She folded the paper and pressed it against her heart, waiting for the guard to return. Her heart throbbed heavy inside her chest as she revisited memories of a happy past. All too soon, the guard came, picked up the letter and returned her to the interrogation room.

"Have you come to your senses?" Kriminalassistent Heller asked.

"Sir, I don't know what you want me to say…"

"Still nothing to say for yourself?" He paced back and forth in front of her, slapping his leg with a leather quirt. "Now is the time to speak up. Give me the names of your contacts in the resistance and you can go free."

Lotte yearned to save her life, but she couldn't do so by sending others to their deaths. "I'm not a spy. I never knew anyone who worked for the Polish resistance."

Heller cursed and yelled, "Take her to the firing squad!"

Two strong hands grabbed her arms and hauled her outside, making her stand facing a stone wall. Below her trembling legs, the ground was damp with the blood of those that had been killed before her. She closed her eyes, willing herself to stay strong in the face of death.

Bullets whizzed past her ears and everything faded to black.

CHAPTER 33

Last days of September 1944

Peter entered the meeting room after being summoned to an emergency meeting with General Bór. He looked around, seeing the room crammed with most every remaining officer in the Home Army.

Colonel Mituk raised his voice. "As you know, the Soviet intervention in the district of Praga was short-lived. After the catastrophic river crossing of Berling's army and the failure to link up with our troops, no more efforts have been made from their side. Bór has personally appealed to Stalin for another intervention, but none has been promised."

A murmur went through the room and Mituk raised his hand to quiet the gathered officers. "It is what it is. We've lost most of our territory and are besieged in the remaining three districts we control: City Center, Zoliborz and Mokotów. All of our units have sustained heavy casualties. The Germans have offered to accept capitulation—"

This time the murmur couldn't be stopped.

"You can't be serious!"

"The Nazi bastards will never comply with any promises given!"

"We might as well shoot ourselves!"

These phrases were only a few of the remarks floating around the room. The door opened and General Bór himself appeared, causing everyone to fall silent at once.

"It is true. General von dem Bach has offered to accept our capitulation and I have started negotiations with his emissaries," General Bór said. "This battle is no longer ours to win. All we can do is fight for acceptable terms of surrender."

"Acceptable terms?" someone scoffed and received a reprimanding glance in return.

"Our main request is that all members of the Polish Fighting Forces, including women and non-combatant persons, will be treated as prisoners of war according to the Geneva Convention and all civilians will be treated humanely," Bórs's right hand, Colonel Mituk, explained.

"I don't think the Nazi pigs know the meaning of that word," one of the commanders murmured, earning nods of several heads in agreement.

Mituk ignored the comment and continued. "Nobody is happy about this outcome, but it's time to face reality. As much as we would like to continue our fight, this battle is lost. We were counting on help from the Allies, or we would never have started this uprising in the first place."

Peter felt sympathy for the colonel. The man was the picture of misery, looking as if he alone shouldered the entire pain of the Polish nation.

"Don't tell your units yet, but make sure they don't engage in reckless attacks. Defend our lines, and retreat when needed. Above all, avoid unnecessary fatalities."

The group dispersed, and Peter set out to find the building that housed his unit. Once he arrived, he could see the failure in their eyes – the hopelessness, mixed with desperate determination. It broke his heart.

In the evening he excused himself and trotted off to visit Agnieska and Jan. They were huddled together in Jan's bed reading a book.

"You here? What's wrong?" Agnieska asked with worry in her voice. He never showed up that late in the evening, because he usually slept in the quarters with his men.

Peter looked at his son, whose face had broken into a huge grin at the sight of his father. For the second time today, his heart broke.

"I want you to leave the city as soon as the possibility arises," he said.

"Leaving? We're besieged," Agnieska murmured. "And we have nowhere to go."

"We are going to surrender."

"What?" Jan shrieked. "But, Dad, you can't."

"We have to. People are starving, and the Home Army is out of weapons. This is the only wise decision." He didn't say that they were also running out of humans to wield the weapons…fatalities had been staggering. Battalions once full-sized had been reduced to a dozen men.

"But...to surrender to the Germans? You'll all be killed," Agnieska said somberly.

"General Bór is negotiating favorable conditions," Peter said, biting his lower lip.

"And if the Nazis don't abide by the terms of the agreement?" Agnieska asked.

Peter didn't have a ready answer for that one. He shrugged his shoulders, hoping against hope the Germans would keep their word.

CHAPTER 34

L otte cracked open her eyes and saw blue skies. *Am I dead already?* A familiar voice reached her ear. *So, he's dead too? That doesn't make sense.*

"Leutnant." Her vicious interrogator, Kriminalassistent Heller, saluted someone with the utmost respect and a clicking of heels. Fear constricted her heart in a vice grip. "We were just about to execute the traitor; you want to watch?"

About to? You already executed me. Lotte craned her head, dizziness attacking her.

"This woman is innocent. We found the real spy," another familiar voice said. One she hadn't heard in a long time. *Is he dead too? I hope not. And why are they talking about me?*

A long silence ensued as the dizziness in Lotte's head slowly faded. Her arm throbbed in pain and once again she tasted blood in her mouth.

Am I still alive?

"So, we're not going to shoot this one?" Heller asked, sounding disappointed.

"No. I'll be taking her with me," the other man responded, obviously pulling rank on the Gestapo officer.

"Let her be. The Leutnant wants to have her," Heller yelled at his men. Stomping footfalls indicated the firing squad leaving the backyard.

Lotte made an effort to pull herself upright. Since she apparently wasn't dead yet, she could at least try to figure out what was happening. She blinked a few times to regain proper vision and then looked directly into Johann's brown eyes. "You? Here?"

"You owe me an explanation," he growled, and helped her up. His touch wasn't gentle the way she remembered it, but he wasn't manhandling her either. Perhaps a tiny sliver of hope remained in this desolate situation.

"I owe you an explanation? Who the hell do you think you are? The Gestapo just tried to execute me," Lotte burst out.

"Watch your mouth. For the time being, I'm your direct superior, and you'd better address me as Leutnant Hauser."

"Aye, Leutnant Hauser," she pressed out between tightened lips. Where had the gentle, serious man she'd fancied gone? In his place was a hardened, angry man she didn't recognize.

They arrived at what seemed to be his office and after locking the door behind them, he turned around, his eyes blazing with rage – and something else. "Sit down."

Lotte obeyed.

"Now, tell me who you really are."

Lotte looked at him, wondering if this was some elaborate trap devised by the Gestapo to trip her up. "You know who I am. I'm Alexandra Wagner."

Johann leaned his hands on the arms of her chair and lowered his face to within a few inches of her own. Anger rolled off of him and stalled the breath in her throat. "Don't lie to me, Alex..." He stepped back and rummaged in his desk, taking out a faded photograph.

Lotte gasped and surged backwards in the chair when she recognized the two people in the picture, her panicked eyes surely giving her secret away.

"Do you know the boy in this photograph?" he asked in a low, threatening voice and answered his own question without waiting for a reaction from her, "Soldat Richard Klausen. And the girl embracing him, do you know her?"

"This is me," she whispered, her heart hammering against her ribs.

"I can see that," he answered, "but Richard told me this is his sister Charlotte, called Lotte."

Lotte tried to control the tremble sneaking up her spine. He had found out her secret. There was no way out, except by telling him the truth. Perhaps not the entire truth, but parts of it. She could only hope that he would understand and not send her right back in front of the firing squad. Seeking any remaining compassion in his brown eyes, she found only fury, disappointment – and hurt.

"It's true. My real name is Charlotte Klausen," she said, observing his face for a reaction. But it remained set in stone.

"Do you know why I have this picture? Because Richard wanted me to give it to his family, should anything happen to him. And you know what I found out? Charlotte Klausen is dead!" he yelled, "Dead! She died from typhus last year in the Ravensbrück concentration camp!" His jugular vein pulsated vigorously, his eyes threatening to jump out of his face.

Despite his rage she put a hand on his arm. "I…I'm not really dead."

"I can see that," he sneered at her, but at least the yelling had been tempered down to a rude loudness.

"I'm sorry. I never meant to deceive you. It was so hard, but I couldn't tell you. If you'd known, you'd have had to report me."

"I still do." His voice lowered to a measured calm, and she believed she saw a glimmer of compassion in the depths of his eyes.

"Why were you at the camp?" he asked, his voice soft now.

She gave the short version of her story. "I got caught hiding a Jewish girl and her baby sister."

"Why on earth would you do such a stupid thing?" He tugged at her arm to make her stand up, but she was no longer afraid of him. The rage drained from his body and he looked at her with the same warm gaze she'd come to love during the past months.

"Rachel was a classmate. When she and her baby sister came to seek my help after their parents had been deported, I couldn't refuse. What would you have done?" She looked at him with wide, pleading eyes.

"They're Jews," he sighed. "We're not supposed to help them." For a moment his eyes reflected his inner turmoil. She knew he'd grown up believing the Jews were responsible for all the bad things that had happened to Germany, but she also knew he owned a kind heart and didn't agree with the atrocious things done to them.

"They're fellow humans. And Rachel was a friend," Lotte whispered.

"It was still a stupid thing to do," he said, rubbing a hand across his freshly shaven jaw, before he tucked a stray lock of her fiery red hair behind her ear. "So why did you become a Blitzmädel? Why not stay in hiding somewhere?"

He leaned near enough now for her to sense his warm breath on her skin. It made her knees wobbly, but this time not with fear. She escaped from the sensation by taking half a step back. "Are you sure you want to know?"

Johann tilted his head to the side, a ghost of his usual smile appearing on his lips. "I guess I already know. You really are a spy, aren't you?"

His declaration stunned Lotte speechless. It took her a while to form her next sentence. "Why did you save me when you know?"

"Because I love you, Alexandra, or whoever you are." He pulled her into his arms and pressed a passionate kiss on her lips. While she was still confused about her feelings for him, his passionate kiss made her realize she was still alive.

Alive!

And he had rescued her. A deep gratefulness coursed through her body and soul, threatening to sweep her away. She clung to him like they were the only two people on earth.

CHAPTER 35

On the second of October 1944, General Bór's emissaries signed the capitulation of the remaining Polish Fighting Forces in the German headquarters in the presence of General von dem Bach. The fighting immediately ceased and the next day German forces began disarming Home Army soldiers and taking them prisoner.

Before walking out to lead his men into captivity, Peter went to say goodbye to his son and Agnieska.

"Don't go," Jan begged him tearfully.

"You know I have to go," Peter said. "You need to be courageous and do as your aunt says. Will you be a good boy?"

Jan nodded, wiping the tears from his eyes and flinging himself into his father's arms. Peter crushed him against his chest, holding him tight, never wanting to let go of him again. But life hadn't turned out the way he wanted it to. He'd come to fight for his country and had lost – again. But he couldn't regret his decision to leave the comparatively safe post in Berlin, because coming here had reunited him with his son.

Trembling with suppressed grief, he peeled his son's arms away, and took the small face into his big hands. "Janusz Zdanek. You have been through so much. You can do this. This war isn't going to last very long now. You stay with Aunt Agnieska and the two of you will protect each other."

"But what about you? Will you live?" Jan asked.

"I will surrender with my men and will be taken as a prisoner of war. As soon as I have an opportunity, I'll send you a postcard with the Red Cross." Peter turned and hugged Agnieska. "Take care of yourself and of my boy. I expect to see both of you again."

"Aye, sir," she said with a sad smile and grabbed Jan's shoulder. "We'll cope. We've been through worse. Haven't we?" Jan nodded, and she continued, "If the Nazis are making us leave, we'll go to Lodz trying to find Katrina and Stan."

"Goodbye." Peter fled the apartment before his beloved ones could see the sole tear slipping down his cheek.

The Home Army had been given two days to gather and march out of Warsaw to lay down their arms. Peter explained to his men the process stipulated in the agreement for the cessation of hostilities and ended his speech with the following words. "Despite the Germans' signing the agreement, nobody knows for sure what they will do. It's a risk we have to take. And make no mistake; being a prisoner of war isn't jolly fun. You'll most likely be forced into labor for them. Food will be scarce, treatment harsh."

Peter spoke from experience. During his time as a driver

for Professor Scherer he'd visited many camps, some better than others, none a place any person would choose to be. He took a deep breath before he said what lay heavy on his heart. "I will not hold it against anyone who wants to take a chance. If you feel your odds are better here, by all means go into hiding."

"What are you going to do, sir?" one of the soldiers asked.

"As your commanding officer, it is my duty to surrender according to the agreement. But…Poland has a need for fighters. The upcoming times will be hard. We've all heard about what happened with the Home Army after liberation by the Soviets. Nevertheless, there's still hope for our beloved fatherland and when the day comes that this war is won, we need men in place to take over." He met the eyes of each of his men then turned his back on them. "If you are going to leave, do so now."

When he turned back around, over half of his unit was gone, and Peter couldn't blame them. He was bound by his loyalty to General Bór or he'd have done the same.

Lotte stretched her limbs and glanced over at Johann lying beside her in the bed. It felt good not to lie to him anymore. He'd insisted on continuing to call her Alexandra, even in private, because he was terrified of letting her real name slip and endangering both of their lives.

She didn't care what name he used, as long as he loved her. A lazy smile crossed her face. She loved waking up in his arms, experiencing a modicum of peace amidst the war-torn city.

"Hey, sweetheart, you're awake?" He kissed her lips and glanced at his wristwatch. "We have about half an hour before I have to get up for work."

"That should be enough time."

She snuggled tighter against him, but he held her at arm's length and said, "I need to talk to you."

"About?" She didn't like the serious tone of his voice.

"I'll send you and Gerlinde back to Germany by the end of this week."

"But why...?" she protested, although she knew his answer already.

"It's too dangerous here. We have no idea how long those stubborn Poles will continue to fight, and then there's the Red Army lurking. I don't want you anywhere near here when they cross the Vistula."

"But I'd rather stay by your side. You'll protect me, won't you?" She traced her finger along his biceps, smiling when goosebumps erupted on his skin.

"That worked out real well last time, remember?"

Of course she remembered the day they'd been captured by the insurgents. "But you saved me from those Gestapo brutes."

"They are brutes, alright, but never call them that, please. You need to be careful." He wrapped his arm around her, finally pressing her against his warm body.

"I am always careful," she said.

Later that morning the news of the capitulation broke and Lotte witnessed spontaneous jubilees. They weren't boisterous celebrations, more like cheers of relief that it was finally over.

After a short time of cheer, everyone burst into activity. Decommissioning of the partisans had to be planned and executed, prisoners taken and transports to POW camps organized. Johann forgot about his plan to send her and Gerlinde away, because he had his hands full taking care of logistics.

Lotte, of course, didn't remind him either. Instead, she and Gerlinde went to see Oberst Braun to be assigned a useful task.

"What the...? Where did you girls come from?" he groaned.

"Sir, I was in captivity and as you know Fräulein Weiler missed the train due to fighting in the area," Lotte said.

"What do you want?"

"We would like to do something useful," Gerlinde said.

"I'm afraid there's nothing you can do. I can't very well assign you the task of disarming the partisans." Oberst Braun looked helpless without Oberführerin Kaiser's help handling all *women's affairs*.

A soldier rushed into the room, skidding to a halt right in front of the two girls with a perplexed look on his face. "Sir, Oberst, we have orders to expel all civilians from the city."

The Oberst groaned saying, "All of them? Half a million or more?"

"Yes, sir." The soldier gazed at his boots.

"How on earth am I supposed to do that with the limited resources at hand?" His glance fell on Lotte and Gerlinde. "Maybe I do have a job for you."

CHAPTER 36

Peter marched his unit down Filtrowa Street in single file, the German standard-issue rifle he'd acquired from a corpse hanging heavily around his neck. According to the instructions they were to carry their weapons without ammunition.

More battalions joined them. As far as the eye could see, a trek of dirty, dejected and depleted men walked towards an unsure future. Most wore whatever ill-fitting civilian clothes they'd obtained, after shedding the coveted *panterka* battle dress. Nobody dared to face the German victors in a stolen SS uniform.

Peter's heart squeezed for all the courageous men shuffling down the broad street. Fifteen thousand, more or less. Every last Home Army soldier who hadn't preferred to seek his luck with the civilians was on the move, adrift on a sea of dirt and desperation.

The days after surrendering were a gray mass of misery. Herded into an open space, exposed to wind and rain, the men waited for their transport to a proper camp. Food was scarce, and optimism was scarcer.

Peter tried to instill a positive mindset into his men, but just looking at the depressed faces made him realize he'd failed. For the insurgents the war was over. They'd seized the opportunity with both hands – and failed. Again. It seemed his entire military career had been nothing but a succession of failures. Although there was no doubt in his mind that he'd do it all over again.

His spirits sank lower with every passing hour as his mind filled with worries about his son and with longing for his wife. He acquired a piece of paper and wrote a letter to Anna.

Beloved Anna,
I'm not sure whether you've been following the news about the uprising. Let me tell you it was an utter disaster. Bloodshed like no other before in history. Myself, I'm awaiting transport to a prisoner of war camp – where, I don't know. I wish I could hold you and kiss you, but this will have to wait until the war ends. For all we know, it might not take long now. Please take care of yourself and stay alive until I return to your side.

He smiled, memories of his time with her flashing through his mind. They'd met not long ago amidst the horrors of war, but still they'd managed to find happiness and peace in each other's arms.

I have met your friend Alexandra. She's well and should have been evacuated weeks ago. And I do have another wonderful bit of news: fate has decided to shine down on me and I've found the son I thought dead. You can't imagine my incredible joy! He's in good care with his aunt, who also miraculously survived. Since Warsaw is in rubble – worse than Berlin – they will travel to the country-side, seeking a safe place to stay.

My heart overflows with love for you and I have missed you every single day. Once this is over, I will never leave your side again.

Love always,

P.

He read the letter again and pressed it to his heart. He couldn't send it to Anna without endangering her. He stuffed it in the pocket of his shirt, where it burned like a hot coal. Maybe once he reached the POW camp he could find a Red Cross worker who'd be willing to send a secret message.

Group after group of Home Army soldiers were shipped off, until it finally was Peter's turn to go. He stood in line with several hundred men, his head bowed in defeat. He actually looked forward to boarding the train. After being exposed to the elements for almost a week, he welcomed having a roof over his head again, even if it was only the roof of a cattle wagon.

"Antek. Piotr Zdanek," a voice called out.

"Yes," he said. The Germans, organized like always, had lists matching the nom de guerre with the real name of the combatants, marking off those transported away. Some-times they'd pull out the odd person they deemed Jewish for further scrutiny.

"Step out," the voice insisted, and he finally looked at the person, only to mutter a curse under his breath.

"What are you still doing here?" he asked in a harsh whisper. "You should be somewhere safe by now."

Lotte cast him a smug grin. She held a clipboard in her hands and moved her pencil down the list, until she found his name. With determination in her face she crossed off his name and wrote *wounded* next to it.

"I'm fine. My gunshot wound is healed," he said.

She kept her eyes trained on the clipboard and murmured, "It's better to be wounded. Trust me. And limp." With a loud voice she added, "Walk with me over there." She grabbed his waist as if he really was an invalid and helped him hobble to a small group of wounded. On the way she produced a tin cup and four packs of cigarettes and slid it into his pocket.

"Thanks." Tears pricked the back of his eyes at her generous gift. Cigarettes were the official currency in the POW camps and could buy about anything. He paused as if he needed to catch his breath from the effort and dug the letter to Anna out of his breast pocket, pressing it into Lotte's hands. "Please, get this to Anna for me?"

Lotte nodded once, tucking the paper beneath the lists on her clipboard. Peter yearned to hug her, but this would be entirely inappropriate and draw unwanted attention to both of them. If the Nazis even suspected they were family, this would bring an array of problems and possibly death for Anna and him. Racial defilement was a crime not taken lightly.

They took up the short walk again and he murmured,

without looking at her, "Can you check up on Jan and Agnieska for me? Please. Take care of my son."

She gave him a single nod, handed him over to the waiting Polish nurse and walked away.

CHAPTER 37

L otte returned to the larger groups of men being loaded onto the trains, trying to rid herself of her tears before anyone else saw them. She couldn't wipe them away without drawing attention to herself, so she kept her head down and blinked them away.

She'd volunteered for this work, but she'd never once thought it would be so gut-wrenching and heart-rending. Thousands upon thousands of defeated and disillusioned soldiers walking into captivity. One look into their dreary faces was enough to make her stomach clench.

Marking down their names on her list, she struggled to ignore that each check represented another human fate. Lotte did what she could to bring those prisoners a tiny bit of comfort. The water bucket at her station was always full, and she reminded every prisoner to drink his fill before stepping onto the train.

Although she believed, hoped and prayed that they'd be treated better than she had been on her journey in a cattle wagon, she was almost sure there wouldn't be enough water to keep their thirst quenched throughout the trip.

The temperature had cooled down considerably in the last days, bringing October rains and heralding the forthcoming winter. With a shiver she remembered her last winter – standing hours and hours in the freezing cold with nothing to wear but her prisoner dress.

Her skin suddenly crawled from the certainty of someone staring at her back and she cautiously turned to see who it was.

Johann met her eyes and approached her, taking her clipboard without a word and running his finger down it until he came to Piotr's name. He glanced to where she had written *wounded* beside it and then met her gaze. "Who was that man? He didn't look injured to me."

Lotte glanced over her shoulder, making sure nobody was within earshot, before she squared her shoulders and whispered, "He is my brother-in-law."

Johann took a few moments to process the information and rolled his eyes before asking, "Any more surprises in your family I should know about?"

"Maybe…" she hedged, not wanting to tell him that her sister, Ursula, had just given birth to a baby whose father was a British bomber pilot. Nor that her nephew Jan had escaped from the Lodz Ghetto…Jan! She needed to find him immediately.

Johann handed the clipboard back to her with a sigh and she followed his strong back with her eyes as he walked away. He might be a Nazi, but he was a good man. Black and white truly didn't exist within the confines of this senseless war.

Her shift dragged on, but at least she had a chance to talk to Gerlinde and find out where the civilians were held. She devised a plan on how to find Peter's son and sister-in-law and then...she had no idea what to do with them, but somehow she'd get them out of Warsaw and to a place of safety.

Johann waited for her after work and together they ate dinner in the mess. It didn't take much coaxing on his part to convince her to follow him to his room. They always tried to be discreet, but nobody really cared. With close to a million people to evacuate, the Red Army still camping nearby, and German soldiers relocated to places of higher priority, everyone was too occupied or too indifferent to enforce morals.

Oberführerin Kaiser would be shocked. Lotte giggled at the thought and opened the door to Johann's quarters. He was already waiting inside for her. He pulled her down onto his bed, showering kisses on her face and tugging at her uniform.

Later, she lay in his arms, in the warm afterglow of making love, and she decided there wasn't a better time to ask him for a favor. She leaned upon his chest and smiled down into his handsome face. "Johann?"

He raised a brow and then sighed. "What do you want?"

"I need a favor," she began, tracing his ear with a fingertip.

"A favor?"

"Just a small one." She put her fingers together in a gesture to show how small. "I have a nephew living here in Warsaw...I would like to take him to Berlin and leave him with Anna and Mutter."

"A nephew? How come I haven't heard about him before?"

"You hadn't heard about my brother-in-law before either," Lotte said, putting little kisses on his chest.

"So, this nephew, does he have a name?"

"He does." She traced her tongue across his skin. "But he cannot use it."

"Because…" He pushed to his elbows, shooting her a stare. By now Lotte knew that when he had this inquisitive look on his face, she'd better tell the truth or come up with a real good explanation.

"…because it's a Polish name."

"I figured as much. But if you want me to help you, you need to trust me with the truth."

Lotte sighed and cast him a pleading look. "I do trust you, believe me I do, but sometimes I think it's for the best if you don't know every detail. Just in case."

"The name," he insisted.

"Janusz Zdanek. His mother died years ago, and his father is headed for a POW camp. He won't survive on his own. You know that." She shed a few tears for good measure.

"You know that your tears don't work with me, don't you?" Johann teased her. The man knew her too well already.

"Alrighty then. But I do love him a lot and want to bring him somewhere safe. He's just a child."

"How old is this nephew of yours?"

"Twelve. Not old enough to be treated as a combatant, and without his parents…" She decided not to chance her luck by mentioning Jan's aunt.

"So you thought you'd bring him to Berlin?"

"Yes. I just need a permit for my cousin Jan Wagner to travel with me and Gerlinde," Lotte said, holding Johann's gaze.

"You need a lot more than a travel permit. He needs papers too," Johann said.

"We could say they got lost in the uprising. Everyone will believe it."

"Too dangerous," Johann said, giving her another of his stern looks and her heart sank – until she noticed the smug grin on his face. "But since I have become resigned to the fact that I won't be able to keep you out of danger, I'll see what I can do."

"Thank you so much! I love you." Lotte pressed a passionate kiss on his lips, showing her gratitude in the age-old way. Within minutes, their bodies slid against one another, repeating what they'd done earlier, celebrating life and their love for one another.

CHAPTER 38

German soldiers closed the door of the train wagon
and Peter found a place against the wall to stretch
out his legs. The journey dragged on and he wasn't sure that
Lotte's attempt to help him had actually been all that
helpful.

The wagon was cramped with injured men moaning and
whining, and a putrid stink settled over everything. It only
became worse with time. The man next to him suddenly
rose, his eyes glazing over as he yelled, "Grenades! Take
cover!"

"Where are we going?" Peter asked one of the nurses.
Doctors and nurses wore the armband identifying them as
Home Army members. The doctors hadn't been given a
choice, but every woman had been allowed to decide
whether she wanted to be treated as civilian or be taken
prisoner. He admired the brave nurses who'd decided to
stay with the wounded soldiers.

"Bergen-Belsen, that's all I know," she said and gave him

a strange look. "You seem to be quite alright. Normally they send men like you to forced labor."

"I have a gunshot wound in my leg," he responded, not wanting to compromise Lotte with a confession.

While he didn't exactly look forward to setting foot in a camp, he did want this hellish journey to end. Several of the wounded had succumbed to their injuries, and being trapped between corpses wasn't exactly a pleasure. Peter reclined his head against the wall, praying for all of this to end. Of course, they'd known there would be dead and wounded. But not this tremendous bloodletting. Close to twenty thousand Home Army soldiers and ten times as many civilians had died.

Had it been worth it? Would it have been worth it, had they won?

These questions tormented Peter. When the train finally arrived in Fallingbostel, a subsidiary camp of Bergen-Belsen, he almost screamed with relief. During his time working for Professor Scherer he'd seen many of the camps from the inside, and he prepared himself for the worst. The minute he set foot into the camp, a wave of gratitude for Lotte's intervention washed over him.

It was ugly, but compared to other camps the Polish barracks were a gem. The treatment when they were unloaded and processed was by far the best he'd ever seen in a camp. Peter was assigned a bunk in one of the huts reserved for the injured and settled into what would become his home for God only knew how long.

CHAPTER 39

With Gerlinde's help Lotte had been inquiring about the whereabouts of Agnieska and Jan. Most civilians had been sent to a transit camp in Prsuzkow, some fifteen kilometers west of the city center, where further selections and distributions were made.

"This could be them," Gerlinde said with excitement, her finger pointing at one of the endless lists. She scrunched up her nose and read the remark scribbled in tiny letters, the enthusiasm fading from her face. "It says Agnieska has been sent for forced labor into the Reich and Jan is destined for Auschwitz."

Lotte tore the paper from her friend's hand, to see for herself. It was the horrible truth. Agnieska had already boarded a train to Dresden, while little Jan – without papers or relatives – was supposed to be deported with the rest of the dangerous, useless or Jewish elements to Auschwitz later that month.

"Still looking for Alexandra's cousin?" Johann asked, sneaking up on them.

"We found him," Lotte said with a shrug.

"Then why so depressed, beautiful doll?" Since nobody else was loitering about the office, he pressed a kiss to her lips.

"He's earmarked to go to Auschwitz," Gerlinde explained.

A barely audible hiss left his throat and he waved sheets of paper. "Then you'd better hurry. Here's a travel permit and a temporary identity card for a German national named Jan Wagner."

"You're the best." Lotte didn't care that at any moment another officer could enter the room; she flung herself into his arms.

"I guess I should do this more often." He grinned after returning the passionate kiss.

"I'll go to the *Dulag* camp first thing in the morning – will you cover for me?" Lotte asked Gerlinde.

"Naturally. My shift won't start until noon."

"What if I invited the two of you to have dinner with me in the officers' mess?" Johann asked with a grin and linked arms with the two women.

The next morning Lotte made sure her uniform was immaculate as she approached the gate of the compound, her entire body trembling with nerves.

"What do you want?" one of the young SS men asked.

"I'm here to find my cousin, Jan Wagner. He's been

captured by the partisans and I believe he was mistakenly brought here," Lotte said.

"Look, doll, we wouldn't have any German nationals here. This is a camp for Poles," a second guard said.

Lotte squared her shoulders. She hadn't expected this to be a piece of cake. "I know, but he's without papers and someone might have mistaken him for a Pole." She waved the temporary identity card in her hand. "Leutnant Hauser from the Warsaw garrison was kind enough to expedite new papers for my cousin."

The two men scrutinized the identity card and the travel permit but shook their heads.

"His parents were killed by a grenade and he's the only one left in my family." She steeled herself for her performance, and pushed her lower lip forward.

"You're not going to cry now, are you?" the younger guard asked her in horror.

"But I must find him!" Lotte begged.

"It's not that we're not willing to help," the older one said. "But there's a hundred thousand people in the camp. We can't possibly go and search for your cousin. It could take hours and we can't leave our position unattended that long."

"Oh, I'm so stupid." Lotte pressed a hand to her mouth and batted her eyelashes. "Of course, you have more important things to do. And I wouldn't want to get you into trouble for leaving your post." She cast them a dashing smile. "Why don't you let me in to look for him?"

"Do you have a pass?" The wavering look on his face told her he just needed a bit more of an incentive.

She moved closer to the men. "I'm being transferred to

Norway next week. If I don't drop off the child with his grandmother in Berlin…" Her eyes filled with unshed tears.

"Norway? Is that where they send all the peachy girls these days?" The younger man was obviously smitten by her flirtatiousness.

"Are you trying to flatter me?"

"Maybe," he said with a wink.

"You look quite dashing yourself." Lotte broke out into a huge smile, although she was holding back the urge to vomit at the mere thought of an SS man touching her. But since her flirting seemed to be working, she continued to suffer.

The older guard inspected Jan's papers again and then nodded for the gate to be opened. "Good luck. And be careful in there. Those Poles cannot be trusted."

"Thank you so much. I'll be back before you know it." She smiled and waved at them.

"Anything for a peachy lady," the younger guard said with a jaunty salute.

Lotte slipped through the gate, anxiety crawling about her skin. The terror caused her limbs to tremble and she could barely keep on walking. She hadn't counted on the deep-rooted fear of being inside a camp again. If it weren't for Peter's pleading face when he'd begged her to take care of his son, she would have turned on her heel and run away.

Palms slippery with cold sweat, she took a few tentative steps inside, a fake smile plastered on her face. *How on earth am I going to find him?* But she shouldn't have worried, because out of nowhere a boy came rushing at her, yelling, "Alexandra! You found me!"

She pressed him against her chest, grateful for his almost perfect command of the German language. He didn't even have an accent. Anyone watching would have seen a young boy falling into the arms of a long-missed family member. Pressing a kiss on his hair, she whispered, "You're my cousin Jan Wagner from Berlin in Germany."

He looked up at her with wide eyes, giving a silent nod. The poor boy had plenty of experience with hiding and pretending to be someone else. "My aunt said to stay near to the gate, because that would be my only chance to leave this place."

"A wise person, your aunt. I'm sorry she was sent away." She grabbed his hand and pulled him toward the gate. Her own hand felt icy against his warm one. She closed her eyes for a moment, mustering confidence and willing away the images of whip-cracking guards.

"You don't have to be afraid," he whispered. "I know what to do."

"I found my cousin," she told the guards with a ready smile. "Thank you so much for letting me look for him."

The two SS men showed a stupefied expression, but soon smiled at both of them and even gave Jan a sweet.

"*Vielen Dank.*" Jan thanked them in perfect German, not showing the tiniest bit of fear he must be feeling.

On the way to the camp Lotte had caught a lift with a military vehicle, but for safety reasons she opted to return on foot. The long march took them almost three hours, but it gave her the time to fill him in on everything that had happened since she last saw him, and her plans to leave him with Anna and Mutter.

She left him in her quarters and went to work. In the evening she and Gerlinde returned to the small room they shared, finding Jan curled up on the bed sleeping.

"Hey, sleepyhead, I want you to meet a friend," Lotte said.

Moments later a knock on the door indicated the arrival of Johann, who stepped inside the room, glancing between Jan and Lotte and saying, "The family resemblance is striking."

"You think so? I couldn't find any similarity," Gerlinde said, scrunching up her nose and scrutinizing the two of them.

Lotte cast Johann a stare, but he only smirked at her.

"I'm here to tell you that I secured transport on the first train to Berlin tomorrow morning for the three of you. A vehicle will wait outside at six a.m. and bring you to the train station," he said.

Gerlinde clapped her hands and pulled Jan into a hug. "We're getting out of here."

Lotte laughed at her antics and shared a meaningful look with Johann. He took himself off a few moments later to give them time to pack. Not that they had much. It took less than ten minutes to gather all their belongings and the biggest delay was finding a suitable container, since their suitcases had stayed behind when the insurgents captured the dormitory building more than two months earlier.

Later that night she tucked Jan into her bed and entrusted Gerlinde with his care. Then she snuck out of the room and made her way across the courtyard to Johann's quarters. As expected, he was waiting for her and pulled her into his arms the minute she slipped through the door.

"God, I missed you, sweet woman," he murmured, pressing her up against the door and sealing her lips in a hot kiss, before picking her up and depositing her on his bed.

Both of them knew it would be their last night together for a long time, perhaps forever. Thus, they took their time removing each other's clothing, and when they came together, it was as a testimony to the love they had for one another. A promise of a future together.

Before sunrise, Lotte slipped into her uniform and kissed him goodbye. He wouldn't be able to accompany them to the train station because they didn't want to draw attention.

"I'm going to miss you," she said, holding back tears.

"Not as much as I will miss you, but I'm counting on seeing you again soon. I've put in for a furlough just as soon as my job here is done. There's no reason to believe they won't approve it."

"How long?"

Johann pulled her into his arms and hugged her close. "I don't know, but we can get through this."

She tipped her chin up, kissing him and committing to memory the feel of his lips against hers, his unique smell, and the feel of his body against her own. During times of loneliness she would simply close her eyes and remember this moment and it would give her the strength to carry on until they'd be united again.

"You have to leave…."

"I'll go wake up Jan and Gerlinde. Johann…"

He placed a finger over her lips and shook his head with a soft smile filled with love. "Don't say it, my love. This isn't goodbye; it's just a small pause. I'll be with you before you know it. Have a safe trip and get word to me that you have arrived in Norway safely."

CHAPTER 40

Lotte stepped off the train, nostalgia sweeping across her heart. Gerlinde and Jan in tow, she walked through the destroyed city to Anna's apartment on the grounds of the Charité clinic. A golden autumn sun shone down on them, casting Berlin in a warm light, but without the heating the air. At the beginning of November, winter hung in the air.

Several months earlier, she'd thought how much more beautiful Warsaw was than her beloved Berlin. But after what the Nazis had done to Warsaw, even a Berlin in ruins appeared to be the epitome of elegance.

She had phoned her sister Anna in advance to let her know she was coming to visit, but hadn't been able to give details, for fear of the line being tapped. Now the three of them stood in front of the sad and dirty employee housing where Anna lived. Lotte shivered for a moment. She brought her sister – or friend in the official version that Gerlinde and Jan knew – good and bad news.

"Hello Alexandra," Anna said as she opened the door and gave a confused glance at the small group. "Who's this?"

"Anna, this is my coworker and friend Gerlinde, and the young boy is my cousin Jan, whom I rescued from accidentally being deported."

Anna frowned but nodded and invited them inside. Lotte could see that her sister was bursting with questions, but with Gerlinde and Jan listening, she couldn't ask them. In the small sitting room, Mutter was waiting. Lotte longed to throw herself into her mother's arms, but even this she couldn't do in her identity as Alexandra Wagner.

"Guten Tag, Frau Klausen," she greeted her mother instead.

After the introductions were made, Anna found an excuse to leave the apartment together with Lotte to talk in private.

"You saw Peter?" Anna attacked her sister with the question that must have been burning on her tongue.

"Yes I did. It was a hellish battle, but he survived," Lotte answered, watching how relief washed over Anna's face. She hated to put a damper on it with her next words. "He went into captivity. I managed to classify him as wounded and send him to Fallingbostel, a POW camp that belongs to Bergen-Belsen."

Anna blanched for a moment. "And who's this cousin of yours really?"

"Jan?" Lotte giggled. "Don't you know by looking into his eyes?"

"But Peter's son is dead. He was deported to Chelmno two years ago," Anna's voice became soft.

"It's him. His aunt gave payola to the guards to get him off the transport and then she hid him for all this time—"

"So Gerlinde is in fact his aunt?" Anna interrupted her.

"Oh, no. Gerlinde really is my coworker and we'll both be deployed to Norway at the end of this week. Jan's aunt, Agnieska, was sent to a labor camp. Peter begged me to take care of his son should anything happen to him or Agnieska. So I brought him to you."

"To me? You mean…" Anna's eyes became round. "I'm only twenty-two and I'm working all day. I can't possibly care for him…"

"I'm sure between you and his new grandmother, you'll do well. He's a good boy. And besides, he has nowhere else to go."

They walked for a few minutes in silence, before Anna said, "Of course we'll take care of him. Somehow it'll all work out. And Ursula is due to return any day. She'll help, too." Anna stopped and turned to hug her sister. "Thank you for doing this. Now I have at least a part of Peter with me."

Lotte smiled. Everything would turn out just fine. The war would be over soon and then she and Johann would be reunited again. She could wait a few months for him.

The End

Thank you for taking the time to read FATAL ENCOUNTER. If you enjoyed this book and are feeling generous, please leave me a review.

Want to know what happens to Peter in captivity? Click here to preorder **Uncommon Sacrifice.**

. . .

If you're curious what happened to Johann in Shanghai and why he was accused of murder-rape, read **Shanghai Story** by my friend Alexa Kang. It's a fantastic WWII tale in the world's most decadent city in 1936: Shanghai Story

AUTHOR'S NOTES

Dear Reader,

Thanks so much for reading FATAL ENCOUNTER. When I visited Warsaw and the Warsaw Uprising Museum in 2017 I knew that I had to write a story about this courageous rebellion at some point.

And who'd be a better hero than Peter/Piotr whom you already met in War Girl Anna? I liked him so much that I wanted to give him his own story. Peter found the son he thought was dead, and while he's now in captivity, this won't be the last word you hear about him. In fact I'm currently writing UNCOMMON SACRIFICE, which will tell the story of Peter and his brother Stan as prisoners of war. Then, Peter will have to face one of the hardest decisions in his life.

My wonderful beta readers Arlene Foster, Sandra Washburn and Chrystyna Lucyk-Berger nudged me to give a more satisfying ending to this book. Unfortunately I couldn't give Lotte her happy end, because it just wouldn't be realistic. But, you'll read about Johann and her in another book set after the war.

Since so many of you begged me to hear from RAF pilot Tom again, I gave him a short cameo appearance. If you don't know who Tom is and why other readers love him so much, you can sign up to my newsletter and read the free short story about how he was shot down and came to know Ursula: http://kummerow.info/newsletter-2

During the process of outlining and writing Fatal Encounter, I used openstreetmaps to make a map with the historic locations in the book. You can find it at the beginning of this book and get an idea about Lotte, Peter and Johann's whereabouts.

As always, I have stayed as close to the actual historic timeline and events as possible. If you think some of the described events are grossly exaggerated, I can assure you, the contrary is the case. I've glossed over the really awful things.

An invaluable research resource was the Warsaw Uprising website http://www.warsawuprising.com and the Lexikon der Wehrmacht http://www.lexikon-der-wehrmacht.de

The Wola massacre was one of the most horrendous killings during the entire war. In only one week approximately 40.000 to 50.000 civilians were systematically murdered. Most of these crimes were committed by the Kaminski Brigade, also called SS-Sturmbrigade RONA and the Dirlewanger brigade, a Waffen-SS penal unit.

Oskar Dirlewanger was one of the most depraved men in history and it is believed that he was beaten to death by

Polish guards during his time as French prisoner of war in June 1945, his unit was mostly comprised of common criminals, poachers, and prisoners of concentration camps.

Bronislav Kaminski, the leader of the Kaminski brigade was another notorious war criminal, who'd been in prison for criticizing Stalin and later defected to the German side. His unit consisted mostly of Russians and Ukrainians. People who had hated the Polish with all their heart for centuries.

Even today it's not completely clear why Stalin didn't help the Polish resistance. Probably because he feared it would torpedo his plan to take Poland for himself. Roosevelt and Churchill exchanged telegrams many times about how to proceed and while Churchill wanted to threaten Stalin, Roosevelt felt they'd be better served not to anger "Uncle Joe" too much. The Poles were – once again – sacrificed on the altar of the bigger scheme of things.

There were numerous routes through the sewers, mostly for groups of three to four messengers with Jewish girls as guides. But ultimately entire districts were evacuated through the sewers. In the Warsaw Uprising Museum I took a trip through a reconstructed – dry and clean – sewer and it was claustrophobic. How much more awful must it have been filled with stinking putrid soak?

Of course I couldn't have written this book without the help of so many special people. Many thanks go to Anja Matijczak and her mother who checked the Polish words for correctness. As always I want to thank my fantastic cover designer Daniela Colleo from stunningbookcovers.com, my editor Tami Stark, my proofreader Martin

O'Hearn, and JJ Toner who generously offered to proofread Fatal Encounter.

My special thanks go to Major Steven Hartov who graciously agreed to review my battle scenes and the chapter about Tom's airdrop. I learned quite a lot from his comments. He's an author, too, and has written the WWII adventure The Soul of a Thief.

I couldn't have done without the help of all these wonderful people!

From the Ashes (Book 1)

On the Brink (Book 2)

In the Skies (Book 3)

Historical Romance

Second Chance at First Love

Find all my books here:

http://www.kummerow.info

CONTACT ME

I truly appreciate you taking the time to read (and enjoy) my books. And I'd be thrilled to hear from you!
If you'd like to get in touch with me you can do so via

Twitter:
http://twitter.com/MarionKummerow

Facebook:
http://www.facebook.com/AutorinKummerow

Website
http://www.kummerow.info

Printed in Great Britain
by Amazon

42864566R00152